"We all know the power of story. The gr... and he revealed many of the principles of the kingdom of God simply by telling powerful stories. I am so happy that my friend, Rhonda Madge, is sharing a powerful story with us in her new book, *Hindsight*. But I should quickly say this is not just any story; this is Rhonda's story. Rhonda's story is real, relevant, and filled with redemption. As you read her story, you're going to experience a wide range of emotions. At times you will find yourself laughing, and on the very next page you may be holding back tears. I have known Rhonda for many years, and I have had a front row opportunity to watch her give birth to this book. She has been courageous in pursuing this project. She has been courageous in sharing some of the most painful parts of her life in order to give help and hope to others. I am confident that you are going to find a deep reservoir of hope and inspiration as you read. It is a story – a true story – but, more than that, it is also a journey from deception to light and life. Rhonda, thank you so much for allowing every reader to travel with you, and I pray that those readers will find what you have found."

RICK WHITE
PASTOR, RICK WHITE MINISTRIES, INC.

"How can I trust You after what You allowed to happen? This was Rhonda's question to God year after year UNTIL... If you are struggling to really trust and believe God is who He says He is, this revealing and honest story will bring you one step closer to that trust. Your journey may look different, but the destination remains the same: face to face with the age-old question, 'Who do you say I am?'"

STEVE BERGER
SENIOR PASTOR, GRACE CHAPEL

"Hindsight is a page turner of memories, shared to help us find our way into and out of our own stories. For within our chapters are misconceptions and lies that continue to influence us today. Also, within them is the potential for life liberating truth. Think about it, childhood is the foundation of who we are, so if it was wobbly, so goes our lives. Rhonda has risked much to tell her story that she might continue to heal and leave a path for others to do the same."

Patsy Clairmont
Author; "You Are More Than You Know"

"In the age of DIY, many couples will seek out old homes in order to create a gem out of something that has been forgotten, something left on the brink of ruin. We watch, in wonder of the beauty that is to be uncovered, until at last strong bones and an original design are revealed. The book you hold in your hand is a story of the renovation of the heart. It tells of a woman from Bumpus Mills, Tennessee; and of the designer who pursued her in the midst of tragedy; and, lastly, it tells of a pursuit of success wherein the beauty and design for which she was intended is unveiled."

Rebekah Byrd
Adjunct Professor at Moody Bible Institute; Author

HINDSIGHT

HINDSIGHT

Seeing Clearly through the Veil of Deception

Rhonda Madge

ELM HILL

A Division of
HarperCollins Christian Publishing

www.elmhillbooks.com

Hindsight

Seeing Clearly through the Veil of Deception

Published in Nashville, Tennessee, by Elm Hill, an imprint of Thomas Nelson. Elm Hill and Thomas Nelson are registered trademarks of HarperCollins Christian Publishing, Inc.

Elm Hill titles may be purchased in bulk for educational, business, fund-raising, or sales promotional use. For information, please e-mail SpecialMarkets@ ThomasNelson.com.

Publisher's Note: This novel is a work of fiction. Names, characters, places, and incidents are either products of the author's imagination or used fictitiously. Any similarity to people living or dead is purely coincidental.

All Scripture quotations, unless otherwise indicated, are taken from the New American Standard Bible'. Copyright © 1960, 1962, 1963, 1968, 1971, 1972, 1973, 1975, 1977, 1995 by The Lockman Foundation. Used by permission. (www.Lockman.org)

Library of Congress Cataloging-in-Publication Data

Pre-Launch ISBN 978-1-400307081

Library of Congress Control Number: 2018961778

ISBN 978-1-400307098 (Paperback)
ISBN 978-1-400307425 (Hardbound)
ISBN 978-1-400307548 (eBook)

To Troy, Taylor, Austin, Rachel, and Luke

*Your laughter rings in my ears as I recount the many paths
we have traveled together.
I know tears muffled the joy on occasion, but through it all,
you have taught me that God's word is everlasting and true.
Love never fails.*

CONTENTS

ACKNOWLEDGEMENTS

I'm finding it very difficult to find the appropriate words to properly thank the many people who have been instrumental in this ten year journey. Yes—you read that right. Since the first day that God asked me to write a book, I have kicked and screamed, "I can't write!" But in the midst of His chuckles, He simply sent someone else to help me swim in unchartered waters.

Natalie Dendy, what would I have done without you? My ten year journey would have easily been twenty had you not agreed to help me. Your ability to form a timeline and teach me how to write dialogue was nothing short of brilliant. Your insight and direction were inspired by the Spirit. I knew from the first time we met that God had indeed chosen you.

An invitation titled, "On the Porch with Patsy," very well changed the way I saw myself. I knew very little about Patsy Clairmont at the time. Yes, I knew she was an author of many books and extremely funny, but little did I know the Lord would use her in my life in such a dramatic way. One day in her home, she knelt before me and said, "You are more than you know." On the days I wanted to give up, her words rang in my ears. She has ministered and taught thousands of women over the years. None can be more grateful than me.

Patsy was also kind enough to direct me to someone who had worked with her in the past, Anna Floit. I was assured that Anna would edit, while maintaining my voice, and she did just that. Another gift sent from Above.

There are so many friends that I could list. We women need cheer-leaders by our side especially when we need a good push. Amy, Rochelle, Sarah, Becky, Tera, and Patti are the one's who gave me what I needed, when I needed it most—even if that meant a swift kick in the you-know-what. You have read the worst of pages and still encouraged, cried with me until there were no more tears, and told me not to give up. Girls, my heart swells thinking about each of you.

Then there's my sweet, and I might add, very intelligent son, Austin. You have never once complained about helping me edit and re-edit page after page. I'm so thankful that you graduated as an English major! The Lord knew how I needed you to put comma's in the right place before the beginning of time! You have loved your mama well through this journey. Thank you my Little Bud from the bottom of my heart.

I could never have accomplished this without my dear Mother. First of all, I would not have had any humor to contribute without her. You are a guiding light of love and encouragement to our family (plus you make the best fried chicken I ever ate). Hearing your voice everyday is music to my ears. I love you more Mama.

Oh my man, how do I thank you? All I have ever heard from you is, "You can do it!" Our life together has given me much to write about. We are living proof that God can use anyone to accomplish His purposes. It started with you sweetheart. I'm so thankful that you hungered for more of Him and loved me all the more.

My Heavenly Father, may this book speak to the one who needs to hear about your grace and mercy. I love you Oh Lord my strength...

Preface

Most of my life I'd appeared to have everything together. A great career, beautiful clothes, travels abroad, and a man by my side. However, appearances are deceiving. On the inside, I was a festering sore. Difficult experiences left me filled with anger and bitterness, forcing me to pretend to be someone I wasn't. It began at the age of seventeen, when a horrific tragedy changed the course of my life.

Forty years later now, in *hindsight*, I realized most of my life has been guided by the fear of exposure and ever-present fear of death. In reality, I had fallen prey to my thoughts and worries, all of which molded my mind into believing such lies.

The stories in this book happened to me. My hope is that, as you read about my life, you will reflect upon your own. The old saying "hindsight is twenty-twenty" certainly is true. A rearview mirror allows us to see with clarity if we don't fall into the trap of guilt and shame. I had to learn that lesson well.

The question is, can you learn from your mistakes and not continue to wallow in the same ones? I finally found joy when I learned to like myself just the way I was designed. Besides, pretending wore me out.

Are you tired? Do you feel you need to wear a disguise to masquerade the truth? Do anxious thoughts consume you all the time, making you feel less than adequate?

If that's you, I invite you to journey down the road that led me from a dark world into the light, as God removed the veil of deception from my eyes.

ONE

"And He called a child to Himself…"

Matthew 18:2

"Rhonda, bring me Daddy's jeans from that chair in the corner," Mama called from the kitchen.

"Yes, ma'am." I quickly retrieved his pants and took them to her. There was Mama, all of five feet and four inches, her dyed red hair already pinned up in curls for the night, meticulously ironing Daddy's work clothes. She was so pretty, with a smile that lit up every room she walked into.

"Tomorrow is Friday, Rhonda. Daddy will take you to Mama Dora's in the morning."

"Ok, Mama."

"What else is important to remember before I send you off to bed?" she asked.

Without even a moment's hesitation I called out, "Blessed be a peace-maker!" In my five short years, I had heard those words more times than I could count.

Mama smiled and opened her arms wide for a good-night hug, followed up by her familiar tickles. I felt so loved by her.

"Now, go give Daddy a good-night kiss and get to bed," Mama said as she gave me one last squeeze.

1

Daddy could probably hear my small footsteps making their way into the family room. He sat in his comfy favorite chair, resting after his long day. His dark hair was swept to one side, revealing his warm brown eyes beneath. Strong hands, weathered from working outdoors, reached down to pick me up. I could faintly smell the Old Spice cologne on his shirt.

"G'night, baby," he whispered.

I threw my little arms around his neck and lingered, not wanting to let go. There was security within these arms. He planted a big kiss on my cheek, patted my bottom, and placed me back on the green-and-white linoleum floor. I happily skipped away to my bedroom and jumped into bed.

****

It was the spring of 1964 in Bumpus Mills, Tennessee. Bumpus Mills was a quaint, traditional Southern town in which all six hundred people who lived there knew the business of the other 599. I was my parents' only child, and our small, two-bedroom white-frame home was sufficient. Next door to us was the home of my daddy's parents, Mama Dora and Papa Chill. Our homes were nestled on an old country road surrounded by farms, quietly grazing farm animals, and a long stretch of tobacco fields.

Early every morning, Daddy would drop me off on Mama Dora's doorstep on his way to work. Daddy rose early and worked late. He began each day feeding our horses and pigs, then headed to his day job as a truck driver with the highway department. After a full day of driving, he would come home to more work on his tobacco farm. This was his year-round routine.

Mama had worked in a factory since the day she turned fifteen. Her feet hit the floor at five o'clock every morning in order to get us fed, dressed, and out the door. Most days she didn't arrive home until almost dusk. My parents continued this schedule day after day to provide for our needs. Others might say we were poor, but I felt rich from the love we shared.

****

I was greeted each morning of the week with a hug from Mama Dora and Papa Chill, along with the aroma of fresh-baked biscuits; a fond routine for sure. Those little biscuits tasted like warm comfort. Mama Dora would wipe the crumbs off my face and pull forward my long, golden curls so they sat ever so perfectly on my shoulders. Being five years old had its advantages, including being treated to an iced RC cola that she kept stocked in her fridge for those hot days late in the afternoon.

She was always in the kitchen, bustling around in her little dress, her stockings held up over her knees with a rubber band so no one could see. I knew, but I was told not to tell because it was a secret. Mama Dora was a petite woman with gray, short curls that covered her head like small, silver spirals. You always knew when she had just returned from the beauty parlor, because you could smell the permanent wave solution when you hugged her. I never minded.

Just as soon as one meal was over, she would start on the next. Of course, it seemed there was always a casserole to bake for church. Papa Chill, on the other hand, loved to be outdoors. Most days he had on overalls, except for Sundays, of course. You couldn't wear overalls to church. He carried a pocket watch that was securely attached to the side pocket. And if you ever needed a handkerchief, he had one ready. His thinning gray hair was combed way over to the side. This way, it looked like he had more hair than he did, or so he liked to think.

My grandparents were at church whenever the doors opened. Mama and Daddy were really good people, but they never went to church. They always told me that I needed to go, but they took Sunday to prepare for the weekly schedule, which would start all over again the following morning.

Mama would get me up on Sundays, dress me in my little frilly dress, and put on my shiny, black patent-leather shoes. However, one particular Sunday, as she was doing my hair, she found a tick on my head. Oh my, that little thing sure caused a mighty itch. It wasn't a big deal, though, because it happened a lot on the farm. However, this day would be different.

Mama Dora and Papa Chill pulled up into our driveway and I jumped in to the backseat. After arriving, we walked into church and Mama Dora said, "Rhonda, go on now to your Sunday school class."

A picture of Jesus awaited me on a low table, along with a selection of crayons to add my expertise. We got to hear a Bible story and sing songs, too. We five-year-olds made beautiful music. However, we all got quiet when our teacher told us to raise our hands if anyone would like to accept Jesus into their hearts. At that very moment I happened to reach up and scratch my head for the umpteenth time. Suddenly I felt my Sunday school teacher grab my arm and race me down to the altar so that I could be saved. I was not even sure what I was being saved from. Maybe they found out I had taken a piece of gum from Mr. Jim's store. I began crying and hollering because by now I was scared to death. However, the church congregation began rejoicing because they thought I was filled with the Spirit. I wasn't.

That experience didn't bring me to Jesus, but it didn't stop me from going to church, either. I remember sitting in that small, red-brick building every week as a child. I would listen to the sounds of classic hymns accompanied by the piano. Messages about heaven and hell were followed by an altar call, and all I really understood was that if I didn't accept Jesus, when I died I would surely go to hell. End of story.

But that was anything but the end of my story.

It wasn't very long after that ordeal when I had questions about who went to heaven. It started the day Daddy dropped me off at my grandparents' like most other days. The morning began with breakfast followed by fried chicken for lunch. Papa Chill decided that he would take a little nap, because he felt tired. Mama Dora thought she would surprise him with some hot oatmeal cookies for when he woke up. After he had slept quite a while she told me to go and wake him while she removed the fresh cookies from the oven.

I skipped to the bedroom and jumped up on the bed. "Papa Chill, wake up. Mama Dora has a surprise for you!" He didn't move. I ran to the kitchen and told Mama Dora that he wouldn't wake up. She dropped her dishtowel and raced toward the bedroom. I had never seen my grandmother run so fast. I ran to keep up. "What's wrong, Mama Dora?"

I watched my sweet grandmother kneel beside the bed as tears fell from her eyes. It wasn't long before people started to come in the house. I sat alone on a stool, not sure what to do. A lady I didn't know brought a wet washcloth and placed it on my forehead. It cooled my head, but did nothing for my troubled heart.

Then my daddy came. I had never seen him cry before. He started beating his head against the wall. "Please, Daddy, don't," I said.

He knelt down beside me and told me that Papa Chill had gone to heaven to be with Jesus.

After that I would think about him especially on Sundays in church. If Papa Chill was in heaven it must be a really good place.

"Will we get to see him in heaven someday, Daddy?"

"I hope so, Honey."

Two

"...Do not be afraid, or panic, or tremble before them."

Deuteronomy 20:3

It wasn't long after Papa Chill died that I started to go to school at Bumpus Mills Elementary. The bus driver, Mr. Sidney, picked me up from Mama Dora's every day for school, but instead of the big yellow bus that I had dreamed of, he drove his car. There were six of us kids with Mr. Sidney packed in like a can of sardines.

As the car pulled to a stop in front of the school, Mr. Jobe, the principal, opened the door for us. Mama had told me he was the boss of everybody and I needed to do whatever he said, so I did.

To my surprise, my teacher, Mrs. Louise, was a tiny little lady. If I stood on my tiptoes I was almost as tall as her. There were fourteen kids in my class and we would all graduate from eighth grade together. Well, that is, all except one.

I couldn't wait to make new friends; being an only child was lonely. There was one little girl who stole my heart the first day. Her name was Karen, but everyone called her Noobie. Her long beautiful curls, fat cheeks, and eyes seemed to see inside my soul. I wanted to be her "best" friend, even though all the other girls wanted the same thing. I was really sad when I found out that she couldn't play outside with me.

"Why, Noobie? Why can't you run?" She told me her knees hurt really bad.

When I got home I asked Mama, "Why can't Noobie run with me?"

"She has something called rheumatoid arthritis." Mama seemed to know all about it, but I couldn't even say it.

"Will she get better?"

My answer came sooner than expected.

Not long after, Mr. Sidney picked me up to start another day. Our giggles faded in the car as we drew near to the school. All of our classmates were sitting on the steps, crying. I pressed my face against the glass, afraid to get out. Mrs. Louise opened the door and took my hand. Kneeling in front of me, she said, "Rhonda, I have some very sad news; Noobie has gone to heaven."

I couldn't move.

Why were so many of the people I loved going there? I cried myself to sleep that night and the nights following. To make matters worse, I had to go to the place called a funeral home again. It seemed everyone had to go there before they went to heaven. It was the same place I went to see Papa Chill and I hated the thought of going back. It smelled funny. How could some place with so many flowers smell like Mama's cleaning solution?

****

Life moved on in Bumpus Mills. Seasons changed, like they do, and years flew by like leaves in the wind. Age ten seemed to be a pivotal growing-up year. I loved the game of basketball more than anything. Hard work taught me that I could accomplish the desires of my heart if I practiced enough. When I wasn't playing basketball, I was expected to keep the house picked up and start preparations for dinner. Growing up also meant I had to learn about the facts of life. I had rather played basketball.

It was a cold, rainy Saturday morning, and Mama ironed while I ate my cereal. She seemed to think it was the perfect time to tell me about the birds and the bees—as she put it. I sat in silence, not sure what to say, as she explained how babies were made. I thought to myself, *Do people really do that?* Dropping one cannon ball into my little world somehow braced me for the next.

"Rhonda, you are getting old enough to know about these things. As a matter of fact, I might as well go ahead and tell you there isn't a Santa Claus, either."

"Who brings my presents?" I asked.

After finding out she and Daddy had enjoyed this little game over the years, I asked, "Can I go play now?"

I couldn't figure out which was worse—the fact there wasn't a Jolly Saint Nick, or sex. I tried to avoid any alone moments for a long time just in case there was something else she felt I needed to know.

Otherwise, life was rather simple, living on the farm. I continued to go to Mama Dora's every day before and after school. I couldn't imagine going a day without one of her sweet kisses on my cheek. She always made a loud *smack* as she planted her lips on me. There wasn't any question that I was loved, but it became frightening at times to think about someone else in my life dying.

There were times at the end of the day when I stood at Mama Dora's window, watching for Daddy's truck to drive up, that I would have horrible thoughts. Fear would creep over my entire body. Tears streamed at the thought of another death.

If something happened to Mama or Daddy, I would be so alone. Who would take care of me?

Within moments, I felt as though my world was coming to an end. Then the second Daddy pulled into the driveway, all was well once again. Out the door I ran. "Bye, Mama Dora. I love you."

****

Life didn't change much for a couple of years, until 1973. I was leaving Bumpus Mills Elementary School and heading to Stewart County High in Dover. On the first morning of school, I arose early so that Mama could fix my hair before she went to work. I had never felt so pretty, standing in front of the mirror in my new outfit. I paused, looking at myself a little longer than usual to make sure I looked just right. Getting new clothes didn't happen very often.

I was excited and nervous when the big yellow bus pulled up in front of our little house. The driver wasn't nearly as friendly as Mr. Sidney. I sat down on the front seat and heard snickers coming from the back of the bus. I ignored them for the most part. Traveling the curvy, ten-mile road into Dover on that bus kept me occupied. My heart pounded out of my chest as we pulled up to the red-brick school building.

The search began for one of my thirteen Bumpus Mills classmates who I had grown up with, but in a school of over four hundred, that was like finding a needle in a haystack. To make matters worse, I was getting rather distracted. There were guys everywhere. I was like a kid in a candy store, that is, until I saw Paul. I will never forget the moment our eyes met.

Paul was from Bumpus Mills, so of course I knew him. It was his senior year, making him three years older than me. A senior showing interest in a freshman girl caused the butterflies in my stomach to take flight. Or was it because of his beautiful blue eyes and brown, wavy hair? He was serious, yet endearing. Most would say that Paul was a real, down-to-earth guy, but one thing I learned quickly above all else, he loved God.

"So, Sunday it is," Paul confirmed.

"Yes. I'll be there. I would like to visit your church," I responded ever so flirtatiously—if it is even possible to flirt over an invitation to church. This was how our dating began, because Mama and Daddy sternly said that I could not date until I turned sixteen. This meant for two long years, Paul and I continued our courtship without actually going anywhere except to his church and our family living room.

I felt secure with him as we sat in the front room of our house on the old, faded orange-and-brown couch, trying our best to sneak a kiss. Mama didn't make it easy. She seemed to have an excuse to poke her head in the door about every half hour. It didn't matter. We fell in love.

We continued dating even after Paul graduated and started college. Most every weekend, he traveled home so we could see each other. Thankfully, after my sixteenth birthday we were able to leave the house in his green Nova and drive around listening to our favorite eight-track tape, *The Best of Bread*. The taste of freedom was sweet, but it always came to an end at eleven thirty and not a minute later. I never tested the waters to see what would happen if I was late. I was known as "Big Ole Boyd Taylor's girl" for a reason. Plus, I was told almost every day, "You be a good girl or everyone in Stewart County will talk about you."

Sunday mornings were my favorite. After church, Paul's mom would always make a wonderful lunch. The worse part came afterward, when I had to help clean in the kitchen. Not that I minded the work; it just meant I had less time with Paul before he left for school. Good-byes were never easy.

"I'm so excited for the revival at church next week. The visiting pastor is really supposed to be great," Paul said. Memories of revivals were not my favorite, but I would do most anything to be with Paul.

Another week passed quickly and I found myself listening to a preacher unlike anyone I had ever heard. My heart began beating uncontrollably. Tears sprang up in my eyes as I heard how much Jesus loved me. The piano started to play and the pastor asked if anyone would like to ask Jesus into their hearts.

I need to wait. I haven't done anything wrong. Why do I need to be saved? What will everyone think?

Be still, heart. There was a battle raging in my head, yet I felt myself slowly rise from my seat, and placing one foot in front of the other, I made my way down the aisle. This time it was for real, no itchy tick bite forcing my hand. I felt Paul touch my shoulder as I knelt at the altar. After the pastor asked my name, he posed the question, "Rhonda, are you ready to ask Jesus into your heart?"

"Yes, I am."

"Do you believe that Jesus died for you and that He was raised from the dead three days later?"

"Yes, I do."

"Rhonda, welcome to the kingdom of God!"

Was it really that easy? I questioned in my mind.

I couldn't wait to tell everyone, especially Mama and Daddy. Surprisingly, others did not share my joy.

"Mama, aren't you happy for me?"

"Of course I am, Rhonda."

"I'm confused. You don't act like it, and why don't you and Daddy go to church?"

"Rhonda, your dad and I just don't have time. We have to work."

I went to sleep thinking about Jesus. I wasn't going to let others hinder me from what I wanted. The following week, Paul, along with our pastor, baptized me in a small creek. As the congregation gathered on the banks of that little river, "Amazing Grace" echoed through the valley.

****

The year 1976 rolled in, our basketball team was having a great season, and I had Paul. Life was good, or so I thought, until things started to get weird.

One weekend, Daddy had cut back our bushes around our house. That Monday morning as I was leaving for school, he asked if I would pick up the clippings when I got home from ball practice. I knew to do as I was told, so I came home and got busy. The beautiful spring day made the work less burdensome.

An approaching car caught my attention. As usual, I smiled and gave a slight wave of my hand. The car came to the edge of our driveway and stopped. As the driver opened his door, I noticed he was wearing an unbuttoned, sleeveless plaid shirt.

"May I help you?"

Silence. Something didn't feel right.

The stranger stepped from behind his car door and I realized he wasn't wearing any pants. The day mama told me about the birds and the bees didn't prepare me for this moment of seeing a naked man for the first time. As he walked toward me, I knew what he was doing with his private parts was not appropriate. Unsure of what to do, I quickly turned and walked to the front door. Once inside, I peeped out the window and watched him get back into his car and drive away.

Thankfully, it wasn't long before Mama and Daddy got home. As soon as they walked in the door I began going on and on about a naked man, but they couldn't understand what I was trying to tell them. After settling down a bit and explaining what happened, Daddy called the sheriff.

To our surprise, the stranger had exposed himself again to another girl much younger than me, and the sheriff already had him in jail.

"Boyd, since Rhonda is older, could she come in to make a positive identification?"

My anxious parents agreed.

The sheriff said, "He's just a weirdo from out of state, plus it's a full moon. I don't believe it's anything to worry about. If Rhonda says this is the guy, we will charge him with indecent exposure and we will never see him again."

Shortly after, we arrived at the jail. Everyone was rather tense until Mother said, "Rhonda might not recognize him with his clothes on."

Everybody laughed except me. I was guided into a room in which cells lined the walls. In the far cell to the left sat the guy who gave me a glimpse of a dark world I never knew existed until that day.

Of course, news traveled fast to all my friends, and the jokes were rampant about Rhonda seeing a naked man.

As if that wasn't strange enough, two weeks later Mother and I drove into Dover to go to the grocery store. The old Dover Bridge that crossed the Cumberland River always unnerved me with its metal that arched the sky above. I usually slowed to turtle speed, afraid that I would hit the rails.

As we approached the bridge that day, we noticed an old woman climbing over the side. Mama screamed, "Oh my Lord, she is going to kill herself!" Uncertain of what to do, we inched closer. The old lady had already crossed over the side rails and was in a squatted position facing us as she gripped the metal with her hands. She was swinging like a monkey from the wind whipping around her. Her little flowered-printed dress blew, exposing a white slip beneath.

I cried out, "Mama, what are we supposed to do?"

Chills ran over my body as the old woman looked right into my eyes, laughing hysterically. Then in one blink of the eye she dropped to one hand and vanished.

"No!" I screamed.

The sheriff's office was within our sight. We raced there for the second time within a month. Frantically, we explained what had happened. The sheriff told us to follow him. Quickly, he traveled to the edge of the water and retrieved a boat. We watched as he pulled her lifeless body from the murky water.

The haunting look of laughter seen on this woman's face ingrained itself in our minds. It helped when we found out she was a mental health patient who managed to escape from her caregiver and wandered from her home to face death.

On two occasions within a short period of time, I had looked into the eyes of a man and a woman who were not in their right minds. "Why is this happening to me?" I began to ask.

I went to school the following Monday and heard the rumors floating around once again. During class, in front of everyone, a fellow student said, "You sure have weird things happen to you."

I laid my head down on my desk, lost in thought. I knew he was right.

The peek into an unknown world of evil left me breathless. What else could possibly happen?

THREE

"The thief comes only to steal and kill and destroy…"

John 10:10

My heart couldn't wait for the lazy days of summer to arrive. Thoughts of horseback riding with Paul gave me goose bumps. The ring of the phone interrupted my daydreams, but I was pleasantly surprised to hear the voice of the one I was dreaming about.

"Rhonda, I just arrived home," Paul said.

I became excited until I realized the tone of his voice seemed serious. "Is something wrong? You never come home in the middle of the week."

"We need to talk. I will be over shortly."

He picked me up and drove us to his farm in silence. The hug and sweet kiss I had come to expect didn't happen.

"What's wrong, Paul?"

He parked his car and turned to me. "Rhonda, I have met someone."

There was nothing that could have prepared me for those words. I felt sick in my stomach. My river of tears didn't affect him. Distant and cold, his mind was already made up.

"You don't know what you're saying, Paul. You know that you love me. We have planned to be together always. Who is she? Tell me!" I screamed.

"Please don't do this, Rhonda. I don't think I love you anymore. That's all I'm going to say."

"Three years together and it's over just like that? Don't you care that you're breaking my heart?"

He didn't have anything else to say. The ride home was silent, and he pulled into my driveway for the last time. Grabbing the door handle, I started to turn toward him, but I could not bear to look at him.

The heartbreak of losing a first love seemed unbearable at the age of seventeen. I believed he was the man I would marry. What had happened? Who was this girl?

Questions and doubts filled my mind as I cried myself to sleep night after night with Mama trying to console me.

"You don't understand. I loved him! I thought we would get married and now it's over."

What's wrong with me? Was she prettier or smarter? Maybe Paul thinks I'm not good enough to be his wife.

I wasn't sure when this pain would ever go away. Unbeknownst to me, the sting of heartbreak paled in comparison to the calamity that was about to crash headlong into my little world.

****

The previous three years I had gone to church with Paul, but as Sunday drew near, I questioned whether I should go. How in the world could I bear to step foot back into the place we had gone together every Sunday? *Well, I guess I can just stay home with Mama and Daddy. Why do I have to go to church? If they don't go, why should I?*

Not going only made matters worse. I laid around all day feeling sorry for myself. Mama finally said, "You have got to pull yourself together. Don't you know that there are a lot of other young men who would love to go out on a date with you?"

I needed to hear that. I got up and decided that I was going to walk into school the next day and get the word out that Paul and I were done. Mama was right.

It didn't take long, either.

Bruce Jones, a senior with a contagious laugh, walked up to me at my locker. "Hey, I heard you and Paul broke up. Would you like to go out to eat with me on Saturday night?"

I looked into those dark brown eyes and gladly accepted.

Saturday came and I was a basket of jimjams, which replaced the heartache quite nicely.

At the sound of a knock, Big Ole Boyd Taylor answered the door and found Bruce stammering, "I'm here to pick up Rhonda, if that's okay."

Daddy told him to come on in. It was obvious we were both quite excited and anxious to get out of there. I'm not sure who was grinning the most. Mama said to make sure I was home by 11:30 and not a minute later.

We hopped in his shiny black car and headed to the Dairy Dip in Dover, where most everyone went to hang out. I couldn't remember laughing so much in a long time.

"Bruce, you are one of the funniest people I have ever met." I wasn't the only one to think so. He had a gift of making everyone around him have a good time.

We pulled up at my house right at 11:30. As I walked to the door, I felt butterflies stirring inside me that had been dormant for some time. As Bruce reached for my hand to draw me near, I thought I would pass out. He leaned in for a kiss, but he didn't have to lean far. I did my part, too. Is there anything as wonderful as a first kiss?

The next morning Mama let me sleep in later than usual. I didn't mind missing church again. It looked as though I might need my beauty rest after all.

Monday could not come fast enough. Of course, I had to play it cool with Bruce. I couldn't let him know just yet that I thought he was adorable. There was also a meeting after school I had to attend that I was really excited about. I was the state secretary of the Future Homemakers of America, and on this particular day we were holding a state meeting in Clarksville, about an hour away. Mrs. Brigham, my home economics teacher, was also going.

Bruce and I met at the lockers a couple of times during the day and he asked what I was doing the following weekend. My ponytail flipped more than usual. The mourning period was over, or so I thought.

Mrs. Brigham and I arrived at the meeting. I had no idea what to expect because it was my first state meeting. As secretary, I was asked to go to the chalkboard to take notes. Suddenly, a strange numbness came over me. I was unable to write the simplest of words on the board.

"Rhonda, are you feeling all right?" Mrs. Brigham asked.

"Um, yes, ma'am." My discomfort was obvious, as indicated by Mrs. Brigham's concern.

Throughout the event, an overwhelming stirring in my soul told me something was wrong. I could not focus, and to make matters worse, I was standing in front of the entire group, unable to write.

One of the girls from another school snickered that I must be stupid or something. I fought back tears. Finally, the meeting adjourned and I was able to drive home, embarrassed and ashamed. I knew I had let Mrs. Brigham down, too.

I'm so stupid. I shouldn't be state secretary.

I approached the big curve right before my house and slowed my car to a complete stop. What I saw didn't make any sense; nearly twenty-five cars lined both sides of the road. Something was definitely wrong. The numbness turned to nausea.

I opened the car door and sat motionless as two men walked in my direction. I realized it was Paul and my Uncle Henry.

Strange.

As they drew closer, I could see they were both crying. Shaking, I got out of the car. Paul was obviously distraught. Incomplete and irrational questions began to whirl around in my head.

Is something wrong with Mama?

I knew it couldn't be my daddy. He was too strong. Stout. He was Big Ole Boyd Tay—I couldn't finish my thought.

Paul was the first to speak. "Rhonda, it's your daddy."

Gulping for air, I tried to breathe.

"He's been killed."

I felt myself slowly falling to my knees in the middle of the road. "No! Please, no! Not my daddy!" I screamed from the depth of my soul. A hush fell through the valley.

Somehow, Paul and Uncle Henry guided my inert body into the house. I stumbled my way into the family room. Mama was sitting on the couch with a few neighbors, who were trying to offer comfort.

Time stopped as our eyes met. I ran to her and fell across her lap.

"Mama. Oh, Mama, please tell me it isn't true!"

"Yes, my baby, it is. Amos Ingle shot your daddy."

I gasped. I must not have heard her correctly. "What, Mama? What did you say?"

"Rhonda, Amos shot your daddy."

I stood, covered my face with my hands, turned, and walked out the back door, the door my daddy had walked out of so many times as he left our home. I could hear the ringing of his burly laugh in my ears.

It was just the previous night when I'd pinned him to the floor in an all-out tickle war. This strong, powerful man, with just a tiny tickle behind his knee, became putty in my hands. Roars of laughter filled the house, and when he just couldn't take it anymore he resorted to spitting in my hair. Our tickle fight developed into a back-and-forth spittle fiasco with Mama standing in the doorway, shaking her head. Tears of laughter filled our eyes as we lay breathless on our backs, wiping away both spit and tears. *Oh, Daddy.*

Was that to be my last memory with my father? My mind quickly came back to reality. From the back porch, I looked up to the heavens and screamed, "Why, God? Why?" Over and over I yelled, "Why did You take my daddy from me? You could have prevented this from happening!" *How can I trust You, God? I invited You in my heart and You let this happen? How can I ever trust You again?*

I'm not even sure how I made it back in the house. People filled our home just like they did when Papa Chill died twelve years prior. I laid down on my bed, surrounded by friends. Delirious thoughts flooded my mind.

He won't be at my graduation.

He won't walk me down the aisle at my wedding.

He will never meet his grandchildren.

Why, God?

I found myself tormented by the thought, "What if something happens to Mother?" The fear consumed me. What would I do if I were left all alone? *Life will never be the same.*

Dr. Lee walked into my room. I felt the prick of a needle in my arm. The room went dark and so did my world as I knew it.

FOUR

"I am weary with my sighing; Every night I make my bed swim. I dissolve my couch with tears."

Psalm 6:6

*M*urder. The word alone is grim and inspires heinous thoughts. It's difficult for me to even utter the insidious word aloud. I do not believe I'll ever grow accustomed to telling others how my father died. Most people don't even know how to respond.

But it happened. Amos Ingle murdered my father.

As far back as I can remember, Amos was always in need of money. He would come to Daddy looking for work, and my big-hearted father would find him a job on our tobacco farm. He worked for Daddy for a number of years, and on the days when there wasn't any work to be done Daddy just let him borrow what he needed.

Amos was a lanky, somewhat gangly man in his sixties. He usually looked as though he needed to shower and shave, or at least change clothes more often. I never truly felt comfortable around him and that rusty, old red truck of his. There was just something unsettling about him. Mama told me never to be alone around him so I knew she didn't trust him, either.

Thinking back, in the fall of '75, about the same time I accepted Jesus in my heart, Daddy had an entire barn of tobacco burn to the ground. I remember the day well because it was the second time I had ever seen my daddy cry; the other was when Papa Chill died.

I had come home from school and found him lying on the couch.

"Daddy, what's wrong?"

"Baby, my entire crop of tobacco burned today. The barn caught fire. All that hard work was for nothing since I don't have insurance. We needed that money real bad. We may not be able to make ends meet."

I didn't know what to say, so we sat in silence.

At the time, Amos Ingle owed Daddy $75.00, yet continued to ask for more. Because of the loss from the fire, Daddy could not loan him any more money; there just wasn't any more to give. As a result, Daddy went out of his way to avoid Amos Ingle for about eight months.

And for those eight months, Amos Ingle festered—until he snapped.

****

On April 19, 1976, right before the sun crept over the low Tennessee hills, my parents were preparing for their usual long day of work as I still lay sleeping. Amos Ingle entered our home unannounced, catching Daddy off guard. Daddy said, "Amos, you are never to enter our home without knocking. Do you understand?" Amos said he was sorry and left. The day continued as normal for us anyway. Amos Ingle, on the other hand, planned out the events that would change our lives forever.

Later that afternoon, while I was at the state FHA meeting, Daddy was driving home from his job at the highway department. A young man, Allen, rode home with him because he lived just up the road a bit. Allen later explained to us that life seemed good as the cool spring breeze blew across their faces while George Jones sang one of their favorite tunes. However, a loud honk of a horn behind them interrupted their ride. It was Amos.

Allen said Daddy pulled his new, white Chevy pickup over in front of a small church on the side of the road and Amos pulled up parallel to him.

Amos yelled angrily from inside his truck, "Boyd, you owe me an apology!"

Daddy answered, "I'm not sure what you are talking about, Amos."

Before Daddy could even finish his sentence, Amos Ingle raised a shotgun from the seat of his truck.

I can't imagine what Daddy must have been thinking as he looked down the double barrel of that gun. *Did you have time to think about Mama and me? Did you cry out to God, Daddy?*

I'm sure it seemed like things moved in slow motion. According to Allen, Daddy pushed him to the floor of the truck and hit the gears.

Daddy, why didn't you fall to the floor of the truck, too?

It was too late. Allen said just as Daddy put the truck in drive, Amos placed his finger upon that trigger and pulled. *Click.* The ringing of the shot echoed through the valley. Daddy slumped over the steering wheel, riddled with buckshot. The pellets also hit Allen's glasses; shattered pieces of glass lodged in his eyes. He could smell the lingering gunpowder in the air. Overcome with fear, he did not move or breathe.

Allen heard Amos get out of his truck and walk over to Daddy's lifeless body and say, "Why, Boyd? Why?" Allen said instinct told him not to move as he heard the rocks shifting under Amos's shoes. Lying covered in blood and pieces of glass, Allen pretended to be dead. Amos leaned over him. Allen said he could feel the warmth of his breath upon his neck. Moments seemed like hours. With strained ears, Allen heard Amos walking back to his truck. The engine started. Allen had lain still until he heard the old, red pickup drive away.

Unable to see from the glass in his eyes, Allen called out to my daddy. "Boyd? Can you hear me, Boyd?" No reply. Allen managed to crawl out of the truck and walk to a nearby home.

What Allen didn't know was that Amos had left the scene and driven straight to the police department. He turned himself in, stating he had just accidentally killed his best friend.

Imagine the surprise on Amos's face when the news came in from Allen Page that Amos Ingle had murdered Boyd Taylor.

I tried to open my eyes the next morning, but I felt drugged and could barely move. I wanted to wake up because I'd had a horrible dream and I was afraid to go back to sleep. It *was* a dream, wasn't it? Maybe it would be better to go back to sleep rather than face the truth.

My daddy was gone. He was just forty years old. How could that be? *God took him. Amos Ingle shot him. God could have stopped him. Why didn't He?* I felt like I was going crazy.

I didn't want to face the day, but I came to quickly understand there were things with which I had to help Mama.

"Rhonda, we have to go to the funeral home to make arrangements," Mama said.

My heart sank and I felt sick. I didn't want to go back to the place with the familiar smell of plastic flowers and death. I was a seventeen-year-old thrown into an adult world way too quickly. Was it really just a few days ago when I'd been giggling on a date with Bruce?

There had been too much death in my life already, but nothing could prepare me for a time such as this. I watched Mama make choices of caskets, vaults, and flowers. We decided that Daddy would be viewed and buried in a new gray leisure suit he had only worn one time.

I remember the day he walked in to one of my basketball games, all decked out in his new suit and burgundy shirt. He was grinning from ear to ear, making the dimple in his chin more pronounced. All of us girls whistled, "You are looking good, Boyd Taylor!" He took a little bow. *Oh, Daddy.*

He was the only man my mother had ever kissed. Daddy, at the age of nineteen, asked her to marry him when she was fifteen. Twenty-one years of a marriage that was not always easy. One might say that they grew up together. In my bitter selfishness, I didn't stop to think how scared she must have been.

Then there was Mama Dora, who had to face losing one of her sons. Daddy was one of eight children. All his siblings tried to console their sweet mother with the right words. Before this time, I had questioned before why people say, "I'm so sorry." I came to realize it's because there simply isn't anything else to say.

The moment came when we all entered the funeral home together. I heard someone say to Mama that the casket was beautiful and the yellow roses draped over him were lovely. I didn't notice and I didn't care. There was only one thing my eyes lingered upon.

Once again, I stared death in the face.

Over two thousand people came to that funeral home to tell us how much Daddy meant to them.

A neighbor said, "He was a good man."

"He worked so hard," said another.

"He would have given you the last penny in his pocket."

I loved hearing all these things about Daddy because I knew they were true.

I was quite shocked when Bruce and Paul both showed up at the funeral home at the same time. Paul was overwrought with pain. I knew he loved my father. We hugged. It's funny that the pain of losing him was a distant memory compared to the ongoing torment I was now experiencing.

Bruce didn't say much; his presence was enough.

However, it was a conversation I overheard Mama Dora having with Daddy's sisters that I didn't understand.

She said, "He looks so peaceful and at rest."

"What in the world are you talking about? What do you mean, Mama Dora?" I asked.

She began to tell me a story that I had never heard before. She said when Daddy was twenty years old, he'd attended a revival and walked down the aisle to accept Jesus into his heart. Daddy's mother and sisters were holding on to the hope that even though he never went to church, that he was still saved.

"Are you telling me there is a possibility that my daddy might not be in heaven?"

Doubts. Fear. Anger.

If he isn't in heaven, are you telling me he is in hell? I'm so confused. I can't understand why God would allow my father to be shot and then send him to hell if He is supposed to be a loving God. *God can't be trusted.*

FIVE

"Whoever commits murder shall be liable to the court."

Matthew 5:21

The days following were so confusing. Daddy died on a Monday, and the following Saturday I was supposed to be in the Miss Stewart County Beauty Pageant. I wasn't sure how in the world I could possibly compete. But all of my relatives, even the ones who lived in other states, said they would stay after the funeral if I would go ahead with the competition.

I sat in front of the mirror that Saturday morning as Mother rolled my hair. She kept saying, "Rhonda, you can do this. Your daddy would be so proud of you."

"I will do my best, Mama."

That night I walked out on the stage as the packed auditorium exploded with applause. Surreal. The corners of my lip quivered.

I made it into the top ten. I wanted to be happy, but I felt guilty. How could I be happy? I felt so beautiful in the solid white dress Mama had bought me to wear. She had paid forty-five dollars just for the slip to wear underneath, plus a special bra that cost more than that. She said I needed that bra to give me a little extra. She had made me promise I would never tell Daddy.

"He would have a fit if he knew I paid that much money for a bra."

We didn't have to worry now.

My name was called for the top five. I joined the other four on the stage as I looked down to see all my family lining the front rows. Tears glistened in their eyes, and Mother gave me a thumb's up.

"And the winner is…Rhonda Taylor!"

I was on a roller coaster of emotions. Only two days prior, I was burying my father and now I was on a stage surrounded by fellow contestants covering me in congratulations. *Surely I'm dreaming*, I thought to myself.

The following Monday morning, I walked back into school. It seemed as if society wanted me to quickly move forward as though nothing had happened. No one seemed to understand that I had a gaping hole in my heart. The old saying "Time heals all wounds" was my only hope. At this point, I had one path—to become a world-class actress.

Of course distractions, such as Bruce, helped keep me busy and my mind occupied. Timing was not ideal for a budding romance. I'm sure he had a really hard time knowing what to say most days, but he continued to make me laugh in the midst of it all.

Bruce and I continued to date through the summer as I prepared to start my senior year of high school and he started college.

It was good to have a boyfriend, and I couldn't wait for basketball season to start. The Friday-night games caused much excitement in small town USA, plus Mother loved to watch me play.

The fall season came and went as winter hastened the removal of the beautiful colors adorning our trees.

Mother and I were learning to live a life with just the two of us. It wasn't ideal, but it was our new reality. When tragedy strikes, you're left to pick up the pieces or the rest of the world moves on without you.

It was hard to believe she was a thirty-seven-year-old widow, married since she was fifteen. She and Daddy had lots of friends, but they were all married and did things with other married friends, leaving her alone.

If I had a date, she would say, "Go have fun. Don't worry about me. I'll be fine." It was hard to leave her sitting alone in Daddy's brown recliner.

The holidays were especially hard that year, not only because we were alone, but looming ahead was the dreadful murder trial.

****

"Rhonda, it's time to go. They're waiting for us at the courthouse," Mama called from the front door.

I glanced at myself once more in the mirror before meeting Mama at the car. I wore a simple dress and curled my hair the best I could, all the while repeating to myself over and over, "I can do this. I can do this."

It had almost been a year since Daddy died. Amos Ingle had spent all that time in the county jail, awaiting trial because bail had been denied. The trial had to be moved to Montgomery County in order to find an impartial jury to give him a fair trial, so it took some time to get this accomplished.

It was a day that we had waited for—to see justice served. We drove in silence as there was not much left to say. I knew I was about to be face-to-face with the man who had shot my father to death.

As soon as my feet touched the floor of the Montgomery County Courthouse, I felt as though I had entered an Alfred Hitchcock movie in the twilight zone. Nothing felt real, except for the tear that slipped from the corner of my eye.

The floor squeaked as we walked. The old hardwoods looked as though they had been installed at the start of the century. I followed the well-worn path to the front row, to a wooden bench that looked like the pews from church. I slid my bottom into place; the cold surface sent a chill throughout my body.

At once, all the anger, anxiety, and grief I had experienced over the past year collided within me. I felt Mother tug at my sleeve, pulling me back into the moment. I lowered my head, trying to conceal the flow of tears.

"Ma'am," a man with a stern voice said, glaring. "If you can't control your emotions, you will need to leave the courtroom."

I can do this. I can do this. No, I can't. No, I can't, I repeated to myself.

"Get a hold of yourself right now, Rhonda," Mama whispered firmly.

The man walked away, satisfied that my mother had taken control of the situation.

I slowly inhaled a deep breath and closed my eyes. As I regained my composure, my eyes cut across to the corner of the courtroom. A door slowly opened and in walked Amos Ingle, handcuffed and accompanied by a court officer. Dressed in gray from head to toe, he walked slowly to his seat with his head bowed. Is this really happening?

"All rise," we were instructed, as the Honorable Sam Boaz entered the courtroom.

The first order of action was to select a jury. Forty-eight were called and questioned before the final twelve and one alternate were chosen. Fortunately, there was not sufficient time to proceed with the first witness.

"We will adjourn until 9:00 tomorrow morning," the judge declared.

The drive home was a silent one. I could tell Mother just needed time to think, as she appeared deep in thought. We both went to bed early in order to start the day rested, if that were possible.

****

Walking back into the courtroom wasn't as bad as the day before, until Mother was asked to take the stand.

I watched her walk as though she were in a trance before taking her seat beside the judge.

"Do you solemnly swear to tell the truth, the whole truth, and nothing but the truth, so help you God?"

Mother answered, "Yes, Your Honor. I do."

She had chosen to wear a black pantsuit that day and her red hair was pinned up in a French twist. Our attorney had told her to dress nicely, but not to wear anything that would draw the attention away from her testimony. The eyes of the jury were upon her as the morning of April 19 replayed from my mother's lips.

"Mrs. Taylor, did you see Amos Ingle the morning of the nineteenth?" the prosecutor asked.

"No, sir. I did not. Boyd and I were both in the bathroom getting dressed when we heard the front door open. He quickly left me in the bathroom to see who had entered our home."

"What time was this, Mrs. Taylor?"

Mother replied that it was 5:30 a.m.

"Did Boyd get upset?" asked the attorney.

She said, "I heard Boyd tell him in a very firm voice that he was never to enter our home without knocking."

The attorney asked if she heard Amos say anything.

Mother said, "Amos replied, 'I'm sorry, Boyd. I didn't mean to upset you.' And then left our house."

"Mrs. Taylor, did you or the deceased have any idea as to why Amos came into your home that morning?"

"No, sir. We had no idea," she replied.

She held it together as long as possible, but when asked about how long they had been married, her shoulders began to shake and tears fell as mother said, "Twenty-one years."

"No more questions, Your Honor."

There was not a bone in my body that would have traded places with her. I knew it was agonizing, yet she managed to do her best. I was so proud of her and I knew Daddy would have been, too.

The prosecuting attorney painted a well-crafted picture of what an outstanding man my daddy was. He had been a good friend to Amos Ingle and even shared vegetables from his own garden with Amos's mother.

Allen Page was called to the stand next. It was not easy for him to recount the memories of that dreadful day. You could have heard a pin drop as he relived the truck ride home with his friend on April 19 of the previous year.

The prosecution rested.

"The defense calls Amos Ingle to testify."

All eyes were upon him as he took the stand. When asked about his relationship with the deceased, he said that Boyd Taylor was a good man and had been a good friend. He testified that he was pawning the gun, because he needed money badly.

"When I lifted the gun to pass it through the window of my truck, it accidentally fired, shooting the best friend I ever had."

The defense said that there were no further questions. Judge Boaz then asked the prosecution if they would like to cross-examine.

"Your Honor, I would now like to introduce the material evidence that Mr. Ingle stated was the gun he was pawning to the deceased, Boyd Taylor."

The attorney leaned over and pulled out the gun.

I stopped breathing at the sight of that weapon.

The prosecuting counsel handed the gun to the foreman of the jury and asked him to pull the trigger. He placed his finger on the trigger, and with great intensity he pulled it back. I shuttered as a loud *click* rattled through the room.

The attorney said, "Ladies and gentlemen of the court, Amos Ingle has indicated that the gun fired accidentally, insinuating that the gun possessed a hair trigger, meaning with the slightest touch it fired." The prosecutor refuted that the gun did *not* have a hair trigger, making it impossible for the gun to fire without any effort. He exclaimed, "The trigger pulled by Amos Ingle was done with force by a man who had a mission, a solitary intent, and that was to kill Boyd Taylor."

It was over. Judge Boaz stated to the jury, "I charge you, members of the jury, that before you find the defendant, Amos Ingle, guilty of any degree of homicide you must be satisfied beyond a reasonable doubt that the death of Boyd Taylor resulted from some unlawful act of the defendant, and was not accidental. Furthermore, the verdict of the jury must be the unanimous, concurring will and agreement of all twelve members. The verdict must not be the result of any gambling or speculative process."

The jury recessed for a short while before the verdict was announced.

The jury reentered the courtroom and all took their seats. Judge Boaz asked, "Have you reached a verdict?"

The foreman replied, "We have, Your Honor."

Judge Boaz asked Amos to stand as the verdict was announced.

"Amos Ingle is found guilty of first degree murder!"

Faint cheers and sighs of relief echoed throughout the courtroom.

The judge sentenced him to ninety-nine years and a day, which meant he was not eligible for parole. Freedom was taken from Amos that day, but it wasn't a give-and-take situation. Yes, justice was served and retribution seemingly occurred, but that did not mean peace found its way into my grieving, angry heart.

"You okay?" Mama asked as we left the courthouse.

"Yeah, I am…um, just glad it's all over," I answered with resolve and an attempt to sound normal.

She pulled me in close to her and whispered, "I love you."

The whole ordeal was finally over. But it didn't change the fact that people whispered when we walked into the local store followed by glances full of pity, daily reminders of our pain. I knew I needed to move on, but I didn't know how. Something in the back of my heart told me I needed God.

But how can God be trusted? He has taken so many people I've loved away from me. Who would be next?

Six

"…And the two shall become one flesh."

Ephesians 5:31

"All right, ladies, two more laps around the gym and practice will be over!" shouted Coach Jobe. The familiar squeaking sound of sneakers pounded the wooden gym floor.

Coach Jobe was the son of my grade-school principal in Bumpus Mills. Everyone knew the Jobe family because they had a reputation of being passionate educators and sports fans. Coach Jobe quickly became a mentor in my life and offered the solid guidance I needed.

As basketball practice ended for the day, I hurriedly gathered my belongings from where I'd left them on the bleachers. Bruce and I had plans that night to see a movie with friends and I needed time to turn from basketball player to girlfriend.

"Rhonda, c'mon here real quick!" Coach Jobe shouted as I was about to walk out of the gym.

I jogged over to him. "Yes, sir?"

He pulled out a photo from behind a notebook on his clipboard. "Who do you think is the prettiest girl in this picture?" he asked. It was an action shot of me during a recent basketball game. I was the only one in the picture.

"I don't know what you are asking because there is no one else other than me," I answered as I squinted my eyes, looking more closely at the photograph.

Coach Jobe pointed to my mother sitting within the crowd. "It's that woman, right there," he said confidently. "What do you think about me asking her out on a date?"

I didn't even have to think about it. Something inside of me was saying it was the right thing. My mother had been so lonely in recent months. She deserved the happiness that a new relationship could bring.

"I think that's a great idea, Coach Jobe," I replied.

He smiled. "Ok then. I'm asking her out."

I drove home thinking about Howard Lee Jobe. He was a handsome, twenty-eight-year-old man who had never been married, and he had eyes for my beautiful mother. He taught history and coached girls' basketball and varsity football for the high school. All the students loved him, even though he was tough when he needed to be.

I laughed aloud, thinking about Mother going on a date with someone nine years younger than her. If he kissed her he would be the second man she ever kissed. I couldn't stop laughing at the thought. I laughed even harder when I realized I had already kissed more than her.

So Howard Lee and Mother began to date. It was almost too much for Bumpus Mills to handle. The widow and the young, handsome coach made pretty hot news. Oh, the gossip. But it didn't seem to bother her much because she was happy and not alone anymore.

We would oftentimes have dates on the same night, posing a problem as she set the same standard for herself as she did for me—home by 11:30. We both refused to be on the porch at the same time, therefore whoever got there first the other had to drive around until the porch dwellers had finished their kiss.

Ah, the front porch—made of old wooden planks slathered with layers of white paint accumulated over the years. It was the place that welcomed you into our home. The same porch I stumbled across trying to find Mama on the day Daddy died. Funny how you never truly understand how much an ordinary place can mean until you realize it has been the backdrop of so many significant moments in your life. Now here we were, Mother and I in a new chapter of our stories, but standing in the same familiar place.

Months of front porch good-byes and good-night kisses eventually led to *two* engagements in the spring of 1977. Ruth and Howard Lee and Rhonda and Bruce were both set to tie the knot.

Bruce and I planned to wed five months after my high school graduation. I strongly believed that marriage was going to fill the emptiness I felt inside. Bruce had walked into my life right after the heartbreak of my first love and the devastation of my father's death. I was ready for a new beginning. Unfortunately, not everyone agreed that this was the best plan for my life.

"I just don't think you're ready, Rhonda. Bruce is a fine young man, but it wouldn't be a bad thing if you had a long engagement. You could go to college and have some fun first."

Mother spent most of the conversation attempting to talk me out of getting married, but I let her words bounce off me, in one ear and out the other. My mind was made up. Nothing she could say was going to change that. I became defensive.

"Mother, I know what I'm doing. You were much younger than me when you married Daddy," I shouted as I stomped out of the room. No one was going to talk me out of marrying Bruce.

The wedding announcement went out in the newspaper, inviting all our friends and family to our fall wedding only four months later.

****

I awoke the morning of my wedding and realized it was actually happening. Fear crept in as I thought about our honeymoon. Growing up, I had been taught that sex was to be saved for marriage and so I had waited.

Then the reality that I was getting married in the church that I had first attended with Paul caused me a moment of sadness. *Stop it, Rhonda,* I told myself.

I heard the phone ring. Mother knocked on my bedroom door and whispered, "Honey, it's for you. It's Paul."

Please, no, I thought. What could he possibly have to say to me?

The first words out of his mouth were, "Rhonda, don't do this. You are making a mistake. Please don't."

"Today is the wedding. I can't back out now."

"Yes, you can," he said. "It's not too late."

"Paul, you ended our relationship because you found someone else. Why are you calling?"

"Rhonda, I know you and I know you are doing the wrong thing."

"I don't want to talk about this anymore. I have to get ready for my honeymoon."

"Please don't talk about that. I can't stand to think about it."

"Bye, Paul." I hung up the phone and sat bewildered. Why had he called?

Mother seemed to have a way of finding joy in difficult situations. Once again, she prevailed. "Rhonda, don't let him hurt you anymore. We have a wedding to get ready for."

"You're right, Mama. Let's do it."

****

Our family and friends gathered at the little church in Bumpus Mills. I waited with my bridesmaids, squeezed into a small room to the left of the entrance to the church. Only a half hour before I was to become Mrs. Bruce Jones, someone lightly knocked on the door.

My Aunt Jeanette walked in as tears glistened her eyes. She knelt down before me, took my hands, and said, "Rhonda, you don't have to do this. We can walk out the door right now. Your Uncle Don and I feel you are making a big mistake. You have your entire life ahead of you. This is the time that you should go to college and have fun. Please don't do it. All your friends just started college and you could be having fun with them."

No one said a word, including me. I loved Uncle Don, my dad's youngest brother, and I valued their opinion, but I wasn't going to call off the wedding. I assured her I was not making a mistake. *This is for the best*, I told myself as I heard the music begin to play through the church hallway.

Uncle Morris, another one of Daddy's brothers, took my arm as we prepared to walk down the aisle—the same aisle I had walked down when I asked Jesus into my heart. What was it about this aisle that caused my heart to beat so rapidly? Two very important life decisions would be made on this faded red rug. To the left of me hung a picture of Jesus, who seemed to be looking right into my eyes. I placed one foot in front of the other as I followed the runner leading to the pulpit. My eyes shifted from Jesus to Bruce.

Am I making a mistake?

I glanced at my bridesmaids, adorned in peach dresses, and searched for assurance. None came. Uncle Morris laid my hand into Bruce's. I wondered if the veil over my face hid the fear in my eyes.

It seemed only moments passed before the pastor said, "I now pronounce you man and wife. You may kiss your bride."

Bruce removed my veil, which had covered my face as a sign of my virginity. He leaned in to kiss his bride. Everyone applauded with joy. I was very thankful I was learning to be a good actress, because I was petrified.

After the ceremony, we gathered for a traditional cake-and-punch reception in the basement of the church. It was obvious that Bruce was ready to get out of there. His groomsmen had decorated the car outlandishly, so after a few good-byes and a tearful hug to Mother, we left for Gatlinburg.

The five-hour drive was not what I had imagined. I never expected my young husband to begin the honeymoon in the car. He couldn't wait to get to our hotel room. Didn't he understand I needed him to be patient and gentle with me? *I am so scared.* I began to wonder why I had gotten married.

It's too late to back out now.

As I prepared to meet my groom in our little hotel room, I questioned why I had not listened to my mother or Aunt Jeanette. Did I really know what love was at the age of eighteen? Did I know how to meet Bruce's needs as a man? No. I did not.

A young girl has such magical dreams about her prince charming and living happily ever after. But I did not feel like a princess when the night ended. My childhood was gone along with my purity. This one act had completely changed who I was forever.

I had stood my ground and gotten what I wanted. I'd heard the old saying my entire life, and it'd never seemed more appropriate than on this day. "If you make your own bed, you have to lie in it."

I closed my eyes and tried to shut out the raging question repeating over and over in my head. *What have I done?*

SEVEN

"For I hate divorce," says the Lord...

Malachi 2:16

It was the day before Thanksgiving 1977, a beautiful fall day in Tennessee, perfect for a wedding. Mother and Howard Lee were all set to become husband and wife. Pure joy radiated from Mother's smile and, well, Howard Lee (I no longer called him *Coach Jobe*) could hardly contain himself. It was a quaint little wedding with just a few family members and friends at a small church in Dover. I watched Howard Lee seal the deal as he planted a big kiss on the woman he had chosen to be his wife. I watched the gravel fly as Howard Lee's new Thunderbird sped off to get him and Mother to the airport on time for their flight to Ft. Lauderdale. I was so happy for her. I missed my daddy, but I knew it was far better for life to be bittersweet than not sweet at all.

As Bruce and I walked back to our car after the ceremony, I looked intently at him. We had been married for nearly three months, and that empty pit I carried around inside me was still yearning to be filled. As I witnessed the bliss emanating from Mother that day, I wondered where my own bliss was. Would true love come with time as Bruce and I grew old together? We, of course, expressed our love for one another, but something was definitely missing.

We had moved to Clarksville, Tennessee, after we married and purchased a very small, older two-bedroom home. Growing up, Mother filled our home with delicious smells and indelible memories, and I looked forward to doing the same with our new humble abode. But as life would have it, we had to pay the bills. So we worked. I got a job as a teller at a local bank while Bruce took college courses throughout the day and worked the second shift at a boot company during the night. We rarely spent quality time together because we hardly ever saw each other. My hopes and ideals quickly became nothing more than empty dreams.

As time went on, I heard less and less from my high school friends. They were all now experiencing college life—dating, going to games, and making new friends. Just being young.

I didn't want to regret my decision to marry Bruce, but I couldn't help but feel an overwhelming sense of loss deep inside. The realities of being an adult *and* a wife brought with them a heavy load. My disappointment and misery began to eat at me.

Bruce was a good guy. He took life one day at a time and assumed everything was fine. But I didn't know how much longer I could keep playing the game of husband and wife. Bruce deserved so much more than what I was willing to put into our marriage.

Funny thing was, no one knew of my unhappiness. I wanted to reach out to my mother, but I was too wrapped up in my self-pride to admit to her or anyone that my life wasn't perfect and that she had been right. So I continued the masquerade.

However, soon I began to taste the fruits of another life. I started making friends at the bank where I worked and we'd routinely meet for drinks when the office doors closed for the day. Since Bruce worked the second shift, I had nothing better to do. One drink always led to another, and before long we'd find ourselves at another bar for just one more.

I'd never really drank alcohol before. I was introduced to several varieties and I found I liked most of them, especially margaritas. Bruce knew about my new friendships and didn't say much. As a matter of fact, he was making a few of his own, which only increased the distance between us.

My new friends were all older than me, a lot older actually, but that didn't seem to matter. As I learned more about them, conversations revealed facts regarding their marriages. Interestingly enough, most had been divorced.

Divorce. That was not a subject I knew much about. As I pondered the realities of my new friends, I realized they seemed happy now. Maybe divorce was my answer.

Divorce doesn't seem like a big deal. Lots of people seem to do it. I could start college and have a new beginning.

****

It was the summer of 1978. I was nineteen years old and on the brink of making another huge life decision.

I was going to leave Bruce.

Just as quickly as I'd made up my mind to get married, I made up my mind to leave. I didn't seek any wise counsel and I certainly didn't pray about it. The lie I had been living would be over and I could focus on my happiness for once. However, I dreaded breaking the news to Bruce. One night I waited up for him to come home from work.

"Bruce, I made a big mistake by getting married. I'm leaving. I'm so sorry."

My dear husband was left in complete shock that night. I blindsided him; he saw none of this coming. He was simply caught in my tangled web of selfishness and deceit.

I drove home to stay with Mother that night. She and Howard Lee were quite surprised to see me that late and knew something must be wrong. They were living in the house where I grew up, right next door to Mama Dora and those endless tobacco fields.

Mother opened the door and I heard myself say, "I'm leaving Bruce, Mother."

She couldn't hide her feelings. I knew the look all too well, the one that says, "I told you so." But she didn't say anything. She just wrapped her arms around me and told me it would be okay. I needed to hear those words.

"Why didn't I listen to you, Mother?"

"Rhonda, we all make mistakes. You are going to have to learn from this and move on."

I cried myself to sleep that night, even though it felt good to once again sleep in my childhood bed.

Why did life have to be so hard?

Where's God anyway?

Doesn't the Bible say that God will never leave you, nor forsake you?

If that's the case, why do I feel so alone?

The sun rose the next morning, offering the warmth I needed. Mother joined me on the front porch with coffee in hand. I braced myself for the coming lecture.

"Rhonda, you are going to have to start life over with a blank slate. I think it would be a good idea to start going to Austin Peay and be with your friends in college as though this never happened." Austin Peay was the local university in Clarksville.

"Mother, do you think it will be that easy?" I asked.

"Well, it will depend on the choices you make. Before you got married, you were a good girl. You will need to go back to that way of life."

I quickly realized she was talking about having sex. "Are you telling me not to have sex with anyone?"

She said, "Yes, *indeed*. That's exactly what I am saying."

I asked her, "Would you buy a pair of shoes without trying them on?"

She spat her coffee out of her mouth. "I can't believe you just asked me that, Rhonda!"

"Well, Mother, sex is important in marriage. I didn't understand all that when I married Bruce."

"Rhonda Taylor, you listen to me. God says we should never have sex outside of marriage."

"Why would I care what God says? He hasn't been there for me. He took Daddy from us."

That was the end of the discussion.

I did want to start over, but I knew I was no longer the same girl who grew up in Bumpus Mills. That happy girl didn't exist anymore.

Unless I pretended to be...

EIGHT

"...For the Lord your God is with you wherever you go..."

Joshua 1:9

I filed for divorce, and in only sixty short days I became Rhonda Taylor once again. I was surprised at how easy it was to dissolve a marriage that was supposed to last a lifetime.

My new lease on life required me to be more independent than ever before. I felt I had to prove something to myself, as well as everyone else. Therefore, I did not move back home, nor did I ask for money from Mother.

I took a job at the Social Security Administration and left the bank behind. I felt gratified after filling out the Austin Peay State University admission application and applying for grants to start classes the approaching fall semester.

My three childhood friends embraced my fresh start on life and invited me to Rush Week, when girls are introduced to the different sororities on campus before classes started.

I moved into a dorm with my new roommate and two suite mates. All three belonged to the same sorority, so of course I wanted to belong there, as well. However, there was a small problem with pledging this sister-hood. Apparently, it was against the sorority's bylaws to allow a divorced woman to pledge. It was as though I bore the Scarlet Letter. *Did I fit in anywhere?* To my surprise, my lifelong friends went before the National Sorority Board and requested special permission for me to be a new pledge. The board agreed. I was the first divorced woman to be allowed in.

The parties that came along with college and sorority life removed the naivety of being a small-town girl. Guys came and went at the rate of a revolving door. My favorite hangout spot was a little pub called the Library. When I told mother that I was going to the library, I wasn't telling a lie.

It became apparent that guys paid a great deal of attention to me as I got older. I learned that with any returned consideration, I had free drinks for the night. A couple of beers usually led to the dance floor. Regardless of where I was, when music started to play, my foot started to tap.

I had learned to dance as a child at the square dances my parents took me to. Of course, high school dances had been fun, too, but I was learning that the rhythm of my body matched the beat of the music in such a way that it became intoxicating to me. Mother would have pulled me off the floor by my ears if she had known.

****

I worked at the Social Security Administration while continuing my college education. I found I enjoyed working. Being raised by two hard-working parents who instilled in me a solid work ethic was paying off.

One of my fellow employees, Lisa, came to me in private one day and said that her husband owned a pharmacy. "Rhonda, he is looking for an employee to work as a cashier and greet the customers. I believe you would be perfect for the job."

"Really?" I said. "I would love that."

Lisa's husband, Andy, interviewed me the next day. He said, "Lisa tells me you have strong people skills."

I replied, "I was raised by parents who taught me to treat others the way I would like to be treated."

I got the job. After giving my two weeks' notice at the Social Security Administration, I started work at the drugstore.

In 1980, I entered into my second year at APSU, pursuing an associate's degree in office management. Unfortunately, all of my partying freshman year meant that my two-year degree would take three years to complete. It was time to buckle down.

It didn't take long for the enchantment of sorority life to wane. Even though they had welcomed me with open arms, the reality was the other girls were on chapter two of their lives, while I felt I was nearing the epilogue of mine. Death, marriage, and divorce had left me riddled with questions about what I was supposed to do with my future.

My confusion only increased after receiving a phone call from Paul, my first love. "Rhonda, I was wondering if you would like to have dinner."

I was shocked and bewildered. "Ok," I answered.

He replied, "I will pick you up at 7:00."

Memories flooded my mind, right alongside the sting of rejection. I wondered if it were possible to turn back the hands of time.

It was good to see Paul. I had changed much more than he in more ways than one. I was no longer the innocent young girl he had loved. We ate dinner and chatted about life in general. Soon, however, the interrogation started.

"What do you want to do with your life? What are your goals? Do you always want to live in this area?"

"I really don't know. I'm trying to figure all that out," I answered. "Can I have a glass of wine, please?" I tried to shock him, but he said of course, even though he didn't join me. Drinking alone was not as much fun.

I didn't like the line of questions coming my way, as it only made me feel worse about myself. *Stupid. Is he purposely trying to make me feel as though I'm brainless?*

I realized there must be a purpose for the questions, but what was it?

Dinner was over. Paul dropped me off at my apartment, leaving me feeling worthless. I suppose he needed to check a box before moving on with his own life, which was confirmed a short time later when Mother called and told me Paul was getting married.

"Their announcement picture is in the paper. This girl is the one he left you for, isn't she?"

Thanks for the reminder, Mother.

****

I began working an average of thirty-two hours each week at the pharmacy. Andy, the pharmacist, approached me one day, saying, "Rhonda, I think you would be great in pharmaceutical sales. You've got the personality, although the position might require a four-year degree. It's worth looking into, though."

I'd never imagined an opportunity as a salesperson would ever come my way. I had seen many of the pharmaceutical reps come in and discuss their products with Andy, but it never occurred to me that I might be able to do that job. *I'm not smart enough for that. It will never happen. Why would they want to hire me?*

I was filled with so many doubts about myself, I had no idea how I would ever regain my self-confidence.

In the spring of 1982, I finished my last semester with eighteen credit hours. Even though I continued to work thirty-two hours at the pharmacy, I was determined to graduate.

One day, a professor of mine called me into her office and said, "Rhonda, I just found out the CEO of Budweiser is looking for a personal assistant. I think you would be a good fit."

"Thank you very much," I replied.

I gave the Budweiser office a call the following week and was given an opportunity to interview. Ironically, Andy had set up an interview for me with Marion Laboratories on the very same day.

What are the chances of that happening? I wondered.

Andy and Lisa became more than just an employer and coworker. They obviously cared for me. Andy asked me every question he thought might come up in the interview and Lisa helped me choose the right outfit. I sensed they understood a career with Marion Labs could change the course of my life.

I walked into the first interview with the CEO of Budweiser. It was far easier than I thought.

He said, "Rhonda, I have one final question and it's probably the most important. Do you like beer?"

"Yes, sir, I do."

He shook my hand and said he would be in touch. Something told me the job was mine.

I didn't anticipate the pharmaceutical interview would be as effortless, but I was wrong. The local rep was actually in town and was asked to do a screening. We chatted and laughed as though we were old friends. He assured me as he left that I would get a call for another interview.

"Great!" I replied.

Two days later I received a call from Budweiser. "Rhonda, we would like to offer you the position of personal assistant to the CEO. Congratulations!" The woman on the other end of the phone told me the starting salary was $14,000.00 and included health insurance.

I had a gut feeling about Marion Laboratories and I knew I was taking a big risk, but I replied, "I'm so sorry, I can't accept the job."

"Excuse me. Did you just decline the offer?" she asked.

"Yes, I did."

I soon wished I'd waited a few days before I told Mother I'd turned the job down. I'm pretty sure she had never yelled at me quite so loudly.

"What do you mean? Rhonda, people don't turn down jobs that pay that kind of money!" she ranted.

Thankfully, the following week I received a call to schedule the second interview with Marion Labs. Mr. Nicol, the district manager, was from Memphis, so we agreed to meet at a local hotel the following day.

I soon began to second-guess myself.

The job with Budweiser was a great job. What have I done? I'm not smart enough to be a drug rep. I'm not going to get this job, and I've already turned down the other one. Why would they want me? I only have a two-year degree and it took me three years to get that.

I felt I was making the right decision at the time, but not now. I tossed and turned most of the night. However, as the alarm sounded in my ear, I arose with a new attitude.

I wore a fitted navy dress with elbow sleeves and a small, narrow belt. I purchased navy pumps to match. Thankfully, my beauty pageant days had taught me how to carry myself with confidence. I held my shoulders back and flashed the Miss Stewart County smile as I entered the room.

Mr. Nicol stood to greet me. He was tall and looked regal in his dark suit. I couldn't help but notice the cufflinks that adorned his monogrammed cuffs.

I shook his hand with a firm grip and sat down, inhaling deeply.

The questions were fairly general as he read from my resume. I was able to avoid telling him I had been married by saying I went to work after high school and worked my way through college. He seemed satisfied with my answer.

We met for one hour and he scheduled a two-hour interview after graduation two weeks later. He said it was necessary to see my transcripts before we met again.

Graduation day came and went and Mother and Howard Lee came to celebrate with me. I could still tell she was worried I had made a mistake by not taking the Budweiser job.

Thankfully, the next meeting with Mr. Nicol came quickly enough.

"Rhonda, your transcripts are quite impressive, especially the last semester. I noticed that you had a slow start, but the part that catches my eye is the fact that your best grades were when you had eighteen hours while working thirty-two. Not many people can do that."

"Thank you very much," I replied.

"This tells me that you work well under pressure, which is a plus. The pharmaceutical industry is fast paced and highly competitive. Do you think you could continue this gait?"

"Yes, sir. I feel certain that I could. I realized during the last semester that the more I had to do, the more accomplished I felt. It was a good feeling."

As we departed, he said he would be in touch. I waited and continued to wait while working at the pharmacy.

Finally, during the second week of August, after waiting three months since my last interview, the call came. Mr. Nicol asked, "Rhonda, what would you think about moving to Little Rock, Arkansas?"

"Little Rock?" I asked with a higher octave than normal. "Really? I've never been to Little Rock."

He explained, "An opening just became available and I would like to officially offer you the position if you are interested."

"Are you kidding? Yes!"

"Rhonda, the starting salary is $18,000.00, and we'll give you a company car, stock options, 401K, and health benefits. Do you think that will work for you?"

I could barely breathe. With tears in my eyes I answered, "Yes, Mr. Nicol. I accept."

"You can call me Bill."

The first person I called was Mother. She couldn't believe it. "You did it, Rhonda. I have to be honest, I had my doubts, but you followed your gut instincts. I'm proud of you, Sweetheart," she said.

Then I called Andy and Lisa. "I got the job! I couldn't have done this without you guys. How do I ever thank you?"

I couldn't believe my good fortune. I knew I had reason to celebrate, but all I could think about was moving to Little Rock.

NINE

"Consider and answer me, O Lord my God..."

Psalm 13:3

Little Rock was far from the fields of Bumpus Mills, miles from front-porch kisses and late-night sorority parties, and just far enough that I could begin a new identity. I was pretty sure my past couldn't follow me across the state border.

I packed up the few things I owned from my apartment and took it all to Mother's. We loaded the boxes in the living room near the spot Paul and I'd sat in for two years, sneaking kisses. A deluge of water had passed under the bridge since then.

A few days later, the moving van arrived to transport my belongings to Arkansas. As the movers carried each box outside, the reality hit me. My family had not traveled much beyond Tennessee, and all of a sudden Little Rock seemed like a foreign country. Mother and I had been through a lot together. How would I ever say good-bye to her? We embraced with the beats of our hearts in sync.

"I love you, Mama."

"Rhonda, I love you more."

"Howard Lee, I'm so thankful she has you. I couldn't bear the thought of leaving her here alone."

We hugged again before I drove away, dreaming about my new beginning.

****

Upon arrival in Little Rock, Marion Laboratories moved me into a hotel and packed my belongings into a storage unit. My first six weeks were divided between Louisville, Kentucky, and Kansas City, Missouri, for training.

Bill, my manager, met me on that first Monday morning and placed three five-inch-thick books before me. I couldn't even pronounce most of the words contained in those pages. Bill instructed me to take the first two days to read through them in my hotel room before I left for Louisville to begin training with a rep in her territory.

All at once the fear from deep within me surfaced, calling into question my decision and abilities.

I can't do this job! I have a degree in office management. Tests are required every other day. I'm not smart enough. Mother told me when I was little that our family weren't book-smart people.

How am I going to be successful? I questioned. Andy seemed to think I could do it, but why? Then I remembered him saying I had good people skills when I worked at the pharmacy. Is that my key to success? He taught me it's not what you say to someone that matters, but how you say it that counts.

The first five weeks went smoothly, but I dreaded the last week in Kansas City where I would meet other new hires. The class I was taking was the first in the history of the company in which there were more women than men, and we were all single. The talking heads gave us a little speech about "looking for love in all the wrong places."

The first day a representative from Brooks Brothers, the clothing store, came to speak to us. We were to dress for success. I was only permitted to wear suits with skirts, stockings, and high heels. Of course, my oversized bobbed hairdo and red-stained lips complimented my conservative daily ensemble.

I didn't say much in class, and if called on I would freeze up. My self-confidence regarding the material I was learning was in short supply, and I was scared to death of saying something wrong. I figured it was best to keep my mouth shut.

On the third day of that week, the trainers divided the group in half for a friendly game. We were placed across from each other with enough space in-between to toss a Frisbee. The object was to see which team could answer the most questions correctly. The Frisbee was given to a person and that person was to throw it to someone on the opposing team. The one who caught it was the person who had to answer the question.

As the other team prepared to throw the Frisbee, I heard, "Throw it to Rhonda. She won't be able to answer it."

I had to plant my feet firmly on the floor in order to keep from running out of the room.

I'm stupid and they know it.

In my emotional state my mind went completely blank, which proved their point nicely. The sales trainer came right over to me and said, "I'm so sorry you were treated that way."

I assured her I was fine.

Once again, I cried myself to sleep that night. By this point in my life, I was used to it.

Friday arrived along with the final exam. It took two hours to finish and my nerves operated in overdrive. After finishing, we trainees left the classroom to take a break, which I desperately needed. When we returned to our seats we found our exams had been returned, with the results face down on our desks. I took a deep breath as I carefully lifted my test paper and peeked on the front side. I'd received a 92%. I had passed the exam and was headed home to Little Rock with great relief. I could not wait to finally move into an apartment and start the process of learning my own sales territory.

It didn't take long to find a one-bedroom apartment nestled on the west side of the city. I enjoyed shopping and buying furniture to set up my new home. Memories came back from when I had tried to make a home with Bruce, but this was entirely different. For starters I had money. It was strange not having to worry about how every dollar was spent. Other than a student loan, I paid rent and utilities. Having a company car was a bonus I didn't fully appreciate until I experienced the benefits firsthand. The company not only paid for the car, but maintenance, gas, and insurance, as well.

Historically, the pharmaceutical industry had been a man's world. There was only one other female rep in the entire state of Arkansas. As I began my territorial rounds, I learned quickly the nurses were overly protective of their doctors. They were used to the male reps making calls and didn't seem fond of a red-lipped, Southern girl finding her way into their offices. I knew if I couldn't get past the receptionists and nurses to talk to the doctors, how would I ever get a doctor to prescribe my product? I had to make friends and make them fast. Mama had always told me the quickest way to anyone's heart is through their stomach, so I fed them. I bought all things chocolate, knowing what women like most. And most assuredly, I confirmed to each of them how important they were.

I burned up the road south of Little Rock, hitting every town with a family practice doctor. We were to visit every doctor once every six weeks, then start the rotation all over again.

****

The first year passed quickly and before I knew it the Marion Laboratories National Awards Meeting was upon us. I didn't expect to win anything, even though Bill had told me about the coveted "Junior Rep of the Year" award.

On the final evening, a black tie dinner and awards ceremony was held. Table seats were assigned, and I found I was the only girl at mine.

The excitement arose within the room as names were called for different accolades.

"The 1984 Junior Rep of the Year goes to the individual that from day one made the decision she would not only work hard, but work smart by building relationships with her customers. This rep has documented success reflected by the sales increase within the territory. It is my honor to present this award to Rhonda Taylor."

I continued to sit in my chair as everyone stood and applauded. Had only one year passed since I had cried for weeks trying to learn the material to sell? Someone shook me back to reality. I staggered to the stage in my new black pumps. Handshakes and pats upon my back left me speechless, but nothing as much as what happened next.

After accepting the award, I walked back to my table to find the sales trainer who had consoled me on that awful day of training, running to me and saying, "You just showed all those reps who made fun of you. You've got the personality that will take you places regardless of how difficult the material is for you to learn. You are a great rep and don't you forget it."

I didn't know how to respond to such encouragement.

****

Snuggled in my bed back home in Little Rock, I awoke to the ringing of the phone at my bedside.

"Hello?" I answered.

"Rhonda, you are going to have to come home next month. A woman called from the State of Tennessee and said they need both of us to go before the parole board in Nashville. Will that work for you, Honey?" Mother sounded concerned.

"I can be there, Mother. You don't think they will actually let him out, do you?" I asked, still half asleep. I sat on the edge of my bed as it was early Saturday morning, and unbeknownst to Mother, I had been out quite late celebrating my award.

"I don't know. I just know he's sick and there's going to be a hearing. So, yes, there is that possibility." The tone of her voice changed from concern to anger.

"I can't believe this, Mother. I'll be there." *This couldn't be good.*

Amos Ingle, the man who intentionally murdered my father six years earlier and was sentenced to life in prison, had developed heart problems while serving time. As a result, he was costing the state a substantial amount of money to pay for his medical care.

****

Mother had been advised to start a petition in Stewart County and gather as many signatures as possible to keep him behind bars. Then together, we would go before the parole board and plead our case.

Dreadful emotions of anger and bitterness came flooding back into my heart. I thought I had left all of my problems and feelings of brokenness back in Tennessee. However, I discovered a person's past can certainly travel across state lines. It seemed my happiness was once again crashing to the ground.

****

Massive, dark buildings loomed before us. Evil seemed to lurk from behind the walls as we entered through the metal doors of the prison. We were treated as criminals ourselves as a security officer padded our bodies down. I shivered as I thought about seeing Amos.

Mother, Howard Lee, and I sat before two men and two women who made up the parole board. I was not prepared to see the man who shortened my daddy's life. Amos walked into the room wearing a pair of jeans and a blue shirt with a number on the pocket. He took a seat at the end of the table at an angle next to me. His cuffed hands clanked as he laid them upon the table. The familiar numbness rushed over my body.

He certainly didn't look sick. He just looked like a slightly older version of the man who had shot my daddy in the back of the head six years before.

The questioning didn't last long. The board members asked Mother a few quick questions and resolutely denied his parole. For the time being, that is.

A few short months later, we were asked to return for another hearing. Again, Amos sat just a few yards away from me. This time, his sister attended, assuring the board that she would care for him and keep him out of any trouble if they would grant his release.

After her plea to the board, Amos turned and looked me directly in the eye.

"Please, please let me spend my last dying days at home with my mother, who is very ill," he begged.

Anger erupted inside of me and I shot back at him, "Why didn't you think about that when you took my daddy from me? I would still have him today if it weren't for you!"

I fought back tears as a kaleidoscope of memories with Daddy rushed through my head. My heart hurt and my anger consumed every inch of my body.

"Parole denied," stated the parole board spokesman.

As we walked out of the hearing, one of the female board members told Mother it was one of the hardest cases they had ever reviewed. It was a battle between what was right judicially and the state's balance sheet.

However, the eventual outcome did not rest on any of our emotions or decisions. Two weeks later, the governor of Tennessee released Amos Ingle. He was free to spend the last days of his life with his dying mother in Bumpus Mills. He passed away a few months later on May 25, 1985.

****

It was hard to believe that I had lived in Little Rock for almost four years. In a short amount of time I had what I most desired: a career, new car, closet full of clothes, stock, and money in the bank. So why did I feel so empty? Where was the contentment I longed for? On Friday nights I traded my suits and stockings for tight jeans, shirts with shoulder pads, bigger hair, and rosier lips to head out for a night on the town, week after week, usually greeted by the same people looking for love.

Monday mornings usually meant packing my car to spend a couple of nights on the road, making sales calls to doctors. This particular week was no different. I packed my bags for El Dorado in order to see a group of physicians bright and early the following morning. The miles passed as the sun lowered in the distance, ZZ Top blasting on the radio.

Suddenly, from behind the wheel of my car, an overwhelming feeling of regret and remorse flooded over me.

Who am I? I don't even know anymore.

I held it together until I pulled into the Holiday Inn for the night. The desk attendant, whom I'd gotten to know well from all my visits, asked, "Are you okay, Rhonda?"

"Yes, I'm just not feeling well. But thanks for asking."

I made it to my room with the familiar flowered bedspreads.

I'll go have a drink. That will help. I don't want to think about my past.

I sat down at the bar and was joined moments later by a guy who wanted to spill his guts to someone who would listen. I couldn't be that person. I had my own stuff to deal with. As I got up to leave, he grabbed my arm and begged, "Don't go." He held on a little too tightly. I jerked away from him and hurried away quickly. As soon as I entered my room the phone rang.

"Can I come and join you?"

I slammed down the receiver and put a chair in front of the door. I called the front desk to let them know a man was frightening me. I didn't hear anything else from him that night.

I threw myself across the sunflowers on the bedspread and wept. I felt as though I was playing a game of tug of war, only I was the rope being pulled and stretched in both directions.

I'm not the girl I used to be! I can never be her again.

I gasped for air. "God? Are You here?" I slipped off the side of the bed, landing on my knees. The ever-present Gideon Bible caught my eye from the corner of the small nightstand. I grabbed it and frantically flipped through the pages, hoping to find words of comfort. None came. I didn't know where to look.

My heart pounded as tears flowed uncontrollably. After what seemed like hours, my cries became a laundry list of questions.

How could God forgive me?

How could He love me after all the things I've done?

Why did You take Daddy from me, God?

"I need to know these things, God!" I yelled out loud, hoping He would hear me.

Holding onto the Gideon, I waited for answers, but nothing came until I awoke the next morning. My first lucid thought was of going to church. I needed answers and surely a church would help. Would a church accept a girl like me?

TEN

"…For the one who doubts is like the surf of the sea, driven and tossed by the wind."

James 1:6

The word *church* was not new to me. After all, it was a place I'd spent every Sunday as a little girl with Mama Dora. I had walked the aisle to accept Jesus with Paul by my side, and it was where I had vowed to be a good wife to Bruce.

However, I was a different person by that point in my life. I wasn't sure how the people would welcome someone like me, a divorcee who didn't trust God.

I walked into a local house of worship that Sunday morning with my head lowered. It was a large church with enough seats for a thousand people, much different from the small country church in Bumpus Mills I was used to. I listened as the choir sang some familiar hymns and soaked in the sounds of God's Word from the pulpit. After the service, the preacher, Brother James, greeted everyone as they left the sanctuary. I introduced myself and asked him if it were possible to meet with him privately.

A few days later, Brother James came to my apartment. I had made up my mind I wasn't going to tell him about Daddy's death and the fact that I blamed God. *That could wait for another day.*

"I need help. I feel like God could never forgive me for some of the things I have done. I got married when I was eighteen and divorced my husband a year later. Since then I have filled my life with stuff I know is not pleasing to God. Will He forgive me?" I asked.

"Rhonda, have you ever asked Jesus into your heart?" Brother James asked.

"Yes, when I was sixteen, but I really haven't been to church since then," I replied.

"Well then, all you need to do is ask Him to forgive you and He will," Brother James assured me.

It can't be that simple. Brother James doesn't know everything. He doesn't know the whole truth. I repeated out loud the words of Brother James. "Jesus, will You forgive me for all my sins?"

Matter-of-factly, Brother James told me I was indeed forgiven and asked if I wanted to join the church.

I was a bit perplexed. "It's that easy?"

"Yep," he nodded. "On Sunday, come forward to the front of the church when I ask if anyone in the room would like to join."

Brother James prayed, shook my hand, and left me alone with my thoughts.

****

While I agreed I would join the church that weekend, I forgot that I was a bridesmaid in a wedding that Saturday night. As the weekend approached, feelings of exhilaration overcame me. I couldn't determine if they were because of the wedding or because I had committed to join the church.

All the bridesmaids met early Saturday morning to have our hair and nails done, followed by a bridal luncheon. My French twist was sprayed stiffly into place. As the time for the ceremony drew near, we gathered at the church, adorned in pink dresses and magnolia flowers in hand, ready to descend down the aisle.

The reception soon followed, and the wedding party hit the dance floor to celebrate our friends' nuptials. After we'd finished off the last of the champagne, the bride and groom drove away in their limo, leaving the rest of us not quite ready to end the night. Someone suggested we move the party to a place called the Wine Cellar.

Live music on the weekends packed the house with folks looking for a good time. We arrived around midnight and I immediately met a guy who knew how to shake a leg, as Mama would say. I was completely disappointed when he said his buddies were leaving and he didn't have a ride home.

"No! You can't leave yet. It's only two o'clock. We can dance for two more hours. I'll take you home."

"You will?" he asked. "I live out in the country, so it's not easy."

"I don't care at all," I replied. And so the dancing continued until four o'clock in the morning. We chatted the entire thirty-minute drive to his house.

He got out of my car and I pulled out of his driveway, the warmth of the heater at my feet. My eyes grew heavy and blurry. I could barely see the road.

"Jesus, if You are here, You are going to have to take this wheel and get me home," I prayed loudly.

I guess He heard me. I awoke on Sunday morning not remembering the drive home, but smelling like a putrid blend of alcohol and cigarettes. Then it hit me—I was joining the church that same morning. I had just enough time to shower and generously spray perfume on Saturday's French twist. Brushing my teeth seemed pointless; I couldn't remove the stale taste from my mouth.

I made my way into the sanctuary and took a seat close to the front. For the next hour I fought to keep my eyes open during the service. Failing once, I nodded off and jerked back awake at the sound of the organ pipes bellowing.

Finally, the invitation to join the church was offered and I slipped from my seat and walked slowly to the altar. Thankfully, I remembered to pop gum in my mouth before going up in front of everyone. Brother James announced to the congregation that I was officially a new member. He then made a request for each person of the congregation to welcome me one by one.

When the sweet church people smelled the combination of my strong perfume and mint gum I'm sure they wanted to turn around and run in the opposite direction. I looked and smelled like the poster child for a lost soul. *I'm not saved. How could I be?*

I drove home, thinking about the joy I had hoped to receive but instead feeling that familiar sense of emptiness. Temporary satisfaction is exactly that—temporary.

Does God talk to people? I wondered. I went back to church the following Sunday and the one after that. I was going through all the motions, but the attendance card at church wasn't filling me up with the happiness I desired.

Going to church just didn't seem to be enough. I'd often wonder, *Isn't there someone who could talk to me and encourage me? I just feel so alone.*

✶✶✶✶✶✶✶✶✶✶

Work kept me busy—actually, extremely busy. One day, my boss Bill approached me about becoming a field trainer. This meant new hires would come to work with me in my territory during their first three weeks with the company.

He said, "Rhonda, your enthusiasm is contagious. It's exactly what we need for new reps to learn. Do you think you can teach others how to build rapport with customers?"

"Bill, you are the one who taught me that the last four letters of enthusiasm are *iasm,* meaning, *I am sold myself.* I would love to be a trainer."

I had every reason to be content and fulfilled, but it seemed I was in a continual search for the one thing that would satisfy my desires.

I'd purchased a new home and that brought some excitement that lasted a few months. When I signed the deed as an owner I felt so accomplished. However, that faded, too.

I'd achieved a mental list of achievements: homeowner, wonderful career, recent promotion, and best of all, church member. The only thing I needed was a husband—or so I thought.

ELEVEN

"It is better to take refuge in the Lord than to trust in man."

Psalm 118:8

Pharmaceutical reps were required to work conventions on average of about three times per year. A large cardiovascular meeting was held in Little Rock in the fall of 1987. Any company that sold a drug pertaining to the heart came to display their information and studies regarding their products. All the cardiologists attended, so it was a great time to visit with them outside of the office setting.

I had bought a new suit for the occasion, dark green with a rather long skirt and fitted jacket to match. I stood at my booth organizing the product brochures, pens, and notepads to give to anyone who stopped by.

I turned around and saw standing before me a handsome man with deep brown eyes.

He asked, "What's your name?"

I extended my hand to shake his and said, "Rhonda Taylor. And you are?"

"Joe. Joe Blackman," he said with a twinkle in his eye. "I just happened to stop by to meet a doctor about some investments. You caught my eye and I wondered if you would like to have dinner tonight."

Again with the twinkle. An invitation such as this had not happened outside of the bar scene in quite some time.

"Dinner would be great."

When my day at the convention ended, I met Joe at a nearby restaurant.

The conversation was easy as I learned more about this Joe who had just walked into my life. He had recently started working in the stock market following three years of service in the military.

He was a man's man who didn't seem to care for small talk. Joe had a stocky build and thick black hair. It was the perpetual smile that highlighted the twinkle, causing my heart to skip a beat. I was smitten.

Things moved rather quickly after that, and a whirlwind romance started. Dinners with good wine and a ski trip to Colorado won me over.

I learned Joe didn't attend church because he didn't believe in God. I was hopeful I could change that. After all, I was the girl who had just sauntered up to the altar and joined a church; surely I was equipped to change this man.

I also realized he didn't have many friends. However, I thought with all of mine, this problem would rectify itself, as well. Still, I was concerned that his only real friend was someone by the name of Sherri who was married to a man named Greg.

We spent a lot of time with Sherri and Greg, going to dinner and dancing. We all shared a lot in common, so the inattention to my friends didn't concern me.

As our relationship became more serious, I took Joe home with me to meet Mother and Howard Lee. The first words from Mother's mouth were, "You're a good-looking devil. I'll say that." Of course, Joe liked the compliment. What man wouldn't?

Later that same night, after Joe went to bed, Mother cornered me in the kitchen. "So tell me, do you think he's the one?" she asked.

"I think he might be, Mother," I replied.

"Give it time, Rhonda. You have only known him for six months."

"Mother, I've learned a lot since being married to Bruce. I think I'm a good judge of character."

"Ok," she replied with those raised eyebrows that suggested she knew something I didn't.

Shortly after our visit, Joe proposed over dinner back in Little Rock. There didn't seem to be any reason to wait to marry, so we set the date for Valentine's weekend, just four weeks away.

The call home to announce the news was received halfheartedly. I knew Mother wanted me to be happy, but in her heart of hearts something worried her.

My second call was to Brother James to ask if he would marry us. He agreed, but thought it would be a good idea to have a couple of premarital counseling sessions first.

I was actually surprised when Joe agreed to counseling, but the level of surprise wasn't as great as when Brother James found out we weren't living together.

"You two live in separate homes and do not plan to move in together until after the wedding?" he asked, shocked.

"That's correct, Brother James," we replied.

He said, "Well, praise God. Most couples today live together first, and I will tell you, it starts marriages off with a disadvantage, oftentimes ending in divorce."

Interestingly, it never came up that I hadn't attended church since I'd met Joe, nor the small detail that Joe didn't believe in God.

He doesn't need to know. What does it matter?

We made the necessary plans to marry in the sanctuary in front of our families and a couple of friends. There wasn't any need for a rehearsal. We were just going to show up.

I wore a tea-length, pale-pink dress with a scalloped hem. It was modest, but perfect for our quaint little wedding. I had my hair cut that day and my hairdresser cut my bangs in the style a two-year-old would wear. Otherwise, I was ready to become a wife again.

This time Howard Lee walked me down the aisle. He asked, "Are you sure this time?"

"I think so. I hope so, anyway."

"Sweetheart, you better know for sure," he told me.

"I promise I am, Howard Lee," I replied as my foot took the first step down the aisle toward the man with the twinkle in his eye.

For the second time in my young life I said, "I do," and Brother James pronounced us man and wife. Joe took my face in his hands and looked into my eyes before he kissed me.

Afterward, we all went back to my house, which would now be *our* house. Champagne was poured and toasts were made as our life began together.

The following morning came early, and we raced to catch our flight to Las Vegas for our honeymoon. I was not aware there would be hundreds of couples marrying in Vegas over Valentine's weekend, but I saw girls everywhere, walking the streets in their wedding dresses after exchanging vows at the local chapels.

I wasn't crazy about Vegas. I had been there many times for various pharmaceutical meetings. It had been Joe's choice to go, and he convinced me that we would have fun.

We only stayed for a long weekend before heading home to settle into married life. After that, Joe worked at home most mornings and I rarely had early appointments, which offered us time to linger over our coffee. We found the weekdays to be fairly routine and longed for Fridays to quickly arrive. Our Friday happy hours were always happy.

We started out inviting my friends to join us, but for some reason everyone seemed uncomfortable, including me. I couldn't put my finger on the reason why, but it meant Sherri and Greg, Joe's best friends, became the only people we'd spend time with on the weekends. My intentions of expanding Joe's circle of friends weren't really working, and neither was my plan to bring him to a belief in God.

****

Over drinks one night, Joe, Greg, Sherri, and I talked about planning a trip to the beach. "Let's do it!" Joe exclaimed. We desired the glimpse of a palm tree and the smell of salt water and simply couldn't wait to get our hands on little umbrella-garnished cocktails.

When we arrived at our destination we raced to dig our toes in the sand and grab our beach chairs. It was then I discovered how insecure I was around Sherri. She always looked so put together, with her slender build and perky blonde hair. Today was no different. The four of us were sunbathing when Sherri jumped up from her chair, offering to purchase the next round of drinks.

"I'm good," I answered as I turned over to even out my tan.

"No, thanks," answered the guys.

"Okay, party poopers. I'll be right back," Sherri said with a wink. As she turned away, she quickly flashed us all, showing much more than necessary—and all in good fun, of course.

Greg and I burst into laughter, but Joe didn't seem nearly as surprised and shocked at her unexpected exposure. My stomach dropped as my laughter quickly turned into a forced smile.

Later that evening, Greg asked me if I thought Joe's reaction to Sherri's flash was odd. We both agreed that they each seemed a little too comfortable with the situation, but there was really no reason to be concerned. *Or was there?* I was comforted, knowing I wasn't the only one who thought their reactions were unusual. I went to the restroom and examined my thoughts. *Can he be trusted?* We'd only been married a few months; he wouldn't have an affair. *Or would he?* They have known each other a long time. *I have to stop thinking about this*, I thought to myself. I pulled it together and rejoined the group.

Joe and Sherri were involved in a conversation, leaving Greg and me on the sidelines. Greg glanced at me and raised his eyebrow. *Oh please, not the eyebrow.* I immediately thought of Mother as my vacation fun fizzled out.

I laid in bed that night determined to remain positive, even if it meant turning a blind eye to the red flags waving in front of me. Why try to fix something I'm not even sure is broken, right?

Joe and I returned home and the memory of sand between my toes faded quickly as we pulled into our driveway in Little Rock. When any of my friends asked about our trip, I pretended that I had fun, even though I couldn't shake the lingering questions in the back of my mind.

Joe and I went through the motions of life with little vigor. Conversations seemed forced and the twinkle had left his eye.

The next Friday rolled around. In the past, before happy hour on Friday afternoons, I'd race home to report my sales calls and do expense reports. It always felt good to have a clean desk before starting the weekend. Joe would leave work a little early to come and pick me up before heading out for the night. But this Friday was different. Five o'clock approached. Then six o'clock, then finally at seven I saw his car lights pull into the driveway.

"Where have you been?" I asked as I looked up from my computer.

"I met Sherri for a drink at Buster's," he replied.

Something pulled at my heartstrings as I said, "I would have joined you. Why didn't you call me?"

"Well, she and Greg have been having a tough time lately and she needed someone to talk to," he said.

The strings twisted a little tighter. *He has been alone with her.* "It doesn't seem right that she would have just asked you and not me. I am her friend, too."

"Rhonda, you know we have been friends far longer."

I bit the inside of my lip and lowered my head, pretending to work again and hoping to indicate that I wasn't pleased with the situation. He got up and went to the kitchen. We spent the rest of the night at home, quietly to ourselves.

The distance between us grew.

****

In the fall of 1988, one year after Joe and I first met and seven months after our wedding, I walked into the house after a day of work. Joe was sitting on the sofa, sipping a gin and tonic. The awkward silence appealed more than the words he was about to say.

"I'm leaving," Joe announced without emotion. He sat the drink on the table and rose to leave.

I stopped, dumbfounded. "I don't understand. I know things haven't been that great lately, but can't we work on this?" I cried.

"I've made up my mind and I'm not changing it. I will be here in the morning with a truck to get my things."

"Joe, we haven't even been married a year."

He walked past me and out the door.

Could I have done something to make him happier? Was I a bad wife? I'd been married twice by now, and regardless of each situation, I knew I was the common denominator. *What am I going to do?* The sofa and a blanket brought some comfort, but I wanted my mother badly.

I dialed her number. "Mother, Joe has left me," I sobbed.

"What do you mean? I don't understand!" she replied.

I told her of his recent behavior and my concerns about his relationship with Sherri. She said, "You need to call Greg and talk to him. Rhonda, have you looked into Joe's phone records or receipts or charge cards?"

"No," I said, "but that's a great idea, Mother." We hung up and I began my search. It didn't take long before the evidence was right before me.

He'd made several long-distance calls to Sherri late at night when he was out of town. I could see how easy it had been because they both traveled. I wondered if they'd been in the same cities.

I called one of my best friends whom I had not seen in a while and she came right over. To my surprise, she had a lot to say.

"Rhonda, I never did trust him. He just had an air about him that he thought he was better than the rest of us."

"Why didn't you tell me?"

"Because you seemed so happy. I didn't want to be the one to disrupt the future you wanted. But I'm not the only one who felt that way. Our other friends did, as well," she confided.

My friend continued, "Rhonda, this may be a blessing in disguise. It's good that you found out what kind of man he is before you had children with him."

She left me to my thoughts. I realized something was telling me to settle this as quickly as possible and not to make him mad. I had seen his temper occasionally and I wasn't sure what would happen if I confronted him about the real reason he was leaving.

After a restless night's sleep, I awoke just as he was supposed to arrive with his moving truck. I looked rough, but I didn't care.

Surprisingly, he rang the doorbell, even though he still had a key. He brought in some boxes and began packing his clothes. We had sold the few pieces of furniture he had before we married, so I knew it wouldn't take long for him to pack what little he had. I sat and drank coffee and watched closely what he was choosing to take without saying a word.

He loaded the pickup truck and slammed the tailgate, indicating that he was done. I walked over and asked for the key.

As much as I tried, I couldn't keep my mouth shut. "You are not fooling me, Joe. I looked at phone records last night, along with American Express charges."

He looked me straight in the eyes and said, "You don't want to mess with me, Rhonda."

Something told me to let him go. He got in the truck and drove away.

On Monday morning, I filed for divorce from husband number two.

Twelve

"…I was brought low, and He saved me."

Psalm 116:6

I sat in my house after filing for divorce the second time, wondering what in the world had just happened. If I could rewind the last fifteen months and go back to the day that Joe stepped into my world, what would I do differently?

First of all, I would have listened to my mother and slowed down the fast-paced romance and looked more closely at the man with the deceitful twinkle in his eye. I'd been so desperate to get married that I placed blinders over my eyes in order to get what I wanted—a husband.

Secondly, he didn't have any friends. Why had I not questioned that more? My mind raced with thoughts of him and Sherri. *How long had they been having an affair?*

Why did he want her and not me?

She's smarter.

She's funny.

She's so thin.

I couldn't take it anymore. I not only felt deceived by him, but by her, as well. I had trusted both of them and they had used me.

Now I was faced with the consequences of my choices. If I wore a scarlet letter after the first divorce, I had just increased the font size of the *A* to cover my entire chest.

What would Brother James say? Would God forgive me again? And the people at home in Bumpus Mills, what will they think of me?

There were so many questions. *Where is Greg?* I wondered. I tried to call him, but he never answered. He and Sherri had been married for a few years. Was she really going to leave him for Joe? Plus, Greg was a very successful man and had provided a lifestyle for Sherri that might not be easy for Joe to keep up with.

Stop this. I can't let this get me down. I've been through worse, I told myself.

I threw myself into work and became reacquainted with my friends, who brought a lot of comfort and encouragement. In sixty short days I would be single again.

****

Halloween fell on a Saturday night that fall and my sales partner, Landis, mentioned that he and his roommate were going to have a party. Landis also lived in Little Rock. We didn't see each other that often, but he was a lot of fun to be around.

"Hey, Rhonda, come over on Saturday night. A bunch of people are coming to hang out. You need to get on with life and quit letting Joe drag you down. As a matter of fact, I think you should meet my roommate Troy," Landis said.

"You have got to be kidding. The last thing I need right now is another man," I replied.

"This guy is different," he assured me.

"Like I haven't heard that before. Has he ever been married?" I scoffed.

"Well, no. But he's a real good guy."

"Why would a really good guy that has never been married before want to go out with someone like me?" I questioned sarcastically.

I could tell Landis's persistence would continue, and since his description of this Troy guy seemed very sincere, I let my guard down a little, even though my divorce wasn't yet final.

"Okay. Maybe I will come, if for no other reason than to just get out of the house," I told Landis.

Guard down, I went to the party. And the first person I met was Troy. Much to my chagrin, we had an instant attraction.

Troy Madge was not only attractive and fit, but he was fun. His thick hair was coal black, which complimented his tanned skin nicely.

I observed him as he socialized with the crowd. *Thank goodness he has a lot of friends*, I thought. He seemed to be great with people. Probably because he, too, was in sales, except in the window-covering industry.

The night ended with what seemed to be mutual intrigue. But I wouldn't jump in with both feet. I decided to tiptoe through the tulips for a while.

A couple of weeks later, two weeks closer to freedom, a friend and I went to the Holiday Inn bar. They had live music and we both needed to get out for the night. As we sat at the bar sipping our cocktails, I heard my name. I twirled my barstool around and was greeted by a huge smile.

"Well, hi, Troy! Fancy seeing you here!" I smiled.

He had a friend with him and the four of us danced until the bar closed. It felt good to laugh and have fun again.

"Hey, would you like to have dinner with me on Saturday night?" Troy asked as we walked to our cars.

Did he know I was still married? I wondered if Landis had told him the details of my life. Surely he wouldn't be interested if he knew.

"I would like that, Troy."

I was excited to see him again, but a little apprehensive, too. I had to tell him the truth about my situation and I couldn't imagine how he'd receive it. We went for a lovely dinner, but I kept looking over my shoulder, wondering what I would do if Joe walked in. After dinner we decided to go back to the house he shared with Landis. I took it as an opportunity to tell him about my past.

I couldn't control the tears as I explained I had been divorced once eight years prior, but as life would have it, I was currently going through a second split.

Minutes seemed like hours before he said anything.

"So? My mom has been married three times," he stated matter-of-factly.

Did this mean he was indifferent to the idea of divorce? At the least, he didn't seem to be judging me, as I had feared he would, but what did marriage mean to him?

The good-night kiss came with a tenderness that I desired desperately. Landis might have been right: Troy did seem different.

We continued dating even though the divorce was still a couple of weeks away. The attorney said it wasn't any big deal unless my ex made a stink about it. I assured him that he had left me for another. I assumed we didn't have to worry about that.

Over the course of dating and long conversations, I learned that Troy had been through a lot in his life, as well. His father had left him and his mother when he was only two years old. His mom then got remarried to a man by the name of Robert shortly after the first marriage dissolved, raising Troy to believe the new husband was his real dad.

Troy recounted stories from his childhood. "I was too young to remember, but Mom has told me about Robert beating me until I was black and blue on the nights he drank too much. He could not drink without getting violent. I'm not sure what I would have done without my mom. She protected me, that was for sure. One night Robert asked me to feed the chickens. Mom said I started crying because I was scared. Robert picked me up over his head to throw me to the ground. Mom screamed at him, 'Put him down right now, and if you ever touch him again, I will kill you!'"

He continued, "Things changed for a little while after Mom delivered her second child, my brother Glenn, when I was four years old. However, it didn't take long before Robert returned to his old lifestyle, hanging out with friends for a few beers. On those nights, we waited cautiously for his return. I remember well the night I stood in the doorway of the bathroom and watched him push my mom's head into a tub of water, then rip her dress off. I was too scared to do anything. Mom never knew I saw that until recently." He lowered his head.

"Then there was the day I won't ever forget. I think I was around ten. I was sick and tired of the way Robert treated all of us. He didn't hit me anymore, but that was because Mom had become his new punching bag. Grandma, Mom, Glenn, and I were in the car headed to Denver to see some family and get away from him. Glenn and I were in the backseat when I told Mom that I didn't want Robert as my dad anymore. She turned around and looked at me, and said, 'Troy, he isn't your real father anyway.'

"I was shocked, yet overjoyed. 'If he isn't my dad, then who is?' I asked. For the first time, I was told the truth about my mom's first husband, my dad."

He continued to explain that it wasn't long after their return from Denver when his mom packed up the boys and moved in with his grandma. He said his grandfather had just passed away, leaving his grandma alone to run the window-covering business by herself. It made sense to support her.

After his mom left Robert, it opened the door for Troy to meet his real dad. He said, "To meet the person who I was supposed to call *Dad* yet knew nothing about was very strange. When I first saw him, all I could think about was how weird his gray hair was. Then I found out that it was a toupee. I couldn't figure out why anyone would choose to have hair that looked like Bozo's, but I couldn't deny he was my father. Without the hair, I felt as though I was looking at myself in the mirror."

Troy's dad had remarried after leaving him and his mom. This woman had a son of her own, and the two of them gave birth to another son named Brian. Unfortunately, this wife died, leaving his father to raise Brian and her son alone.

I became confused. "So you have how many brothers?"

He smiled and answered, "It is confusing. I have a brother from my mother and Robert, who is Glenn. Then I have a brother from my dad and his wife, who is Brian. The other son my dad raised, because his mother died, isn't really related to me. So I have two half-brothers. Make sense now?"

I learned that Troy and Brian had gone on fishing trips together with Glenn. Their big joke was, "Whose brother are you anyway?"

After hearing about his life, I realized this guy was resilient even after facing so much adversity. "Troy, what did you do for fun growing up? Did you play sports?"

"Yeah, sports meant everything to me. I played them all, but football was my favorite. Looking back, I guess a ball served as a distraction from all the craziness around me. Besides, there wasn't much else to do in Sioux City. I was told I was somewhat gifted and driven, which made a good combination."

His story continued to evolve. "We hadn't lived with Grandma for long when Mom started joining her for drinks. The drinking led to nights out, where Mom soon met her third husband. Once again we packed up and moved. This time to a farm across the state line in Nebraska. Our new home was just thirty minutes away from Grandma, so Mom continued to make draperies for the business. Looking back now, a defining moment in my life was when Grandma decided it was time to train me to install the window coverings they designed. It was good money for a fifteen-year-old, so I didn't mind one bit, but what she taught me was invaluable. I learned not only about installations, but the window-covering industry in general, which landed me this career with Kirsch, a manufacturer of drapery hardware. I was given the sales territory in Arkansas, which is how I ended up here."

Troy explained that his mom's third husband was a hardworking man with a big heart. But unfortunately, for unclear reasons, they were only married about five years. Thankfully, those years allowed Troy to start and graduate from New Castle High School.

"Rhonda, you need to understand that my mom and grandma are alcoholics. It's the reason I don't drink to get drunk. I enjoy having a couple of beers, but I don't get drunk because I've seen what it can do to a person."

I wanted to ask him about church, but I hesitated. *Why do I care?* I asked myself. *What does it matter?* In my gut, it did matter. "Do you go to church, Troy?"

"I grew up Catholic, but honestly it's been a long time since I went to Mass. What about you?"

"I joined a church here in Little Rock before Joe and I got married. He didn't want to go, though, so I haven't been back since."

****

The court date to dissolve my second marriage drew closer, and the more time I spent with Troy, the more I liked him. We enjoyed cooking and watching movies together. It was a nice change from the bar scene. With steaks marinating, candles lit, and placemats on the table, I heard a light knock at the door.

It was always great to see him. This particular night seemed more relaxed than others as we put the meat on the grill and sipped our glasses of wine. The stars were shining and the air was crisp. The smell of a neighbor's wood burning lingered, reminding me of home.

We finished up dinner and I cleared the table in anticipation of snuggling on the couch. Troy excused himself to use the bathroom just as the doorbell rang.

Unfortunately, I opened the door without checking to see who it was. I had to think quickly in order to duck and miss the fist coming right at my face. The fist belonged to Joe, and the smell of alcohol on him was strong. I screamed for Troy and ran out into the cul-de-sac with Joe chasing close behind. Troy ran out of the house, and just as he reached me, Joe took a swing at him, too. Fortunately, Joe was still dressed in his business clothes and dress shoes with slippery soles. He lost his footing and fell to the ground, allowing Troy and I to run back inside the house.

We locked the front door and called the police, just as we heard glass shattering from the garage. I was frantically talking to an emergency responder on the phone when suddenly Joe appeared at the atrium doors, kicking the door with all his strength and yelling, "I will kill you both if it's the last thing I do!"

The police could hear his threats and told us they were on their way. As quickly as Joe appeared, he vanished. By the time the police arrived, he wasn't anywhere to be found. As the cops talked and the story unfolded, we realized Joe had probably been sitting in the backyard observing our dinner through the glass doors. Had he been out there when we were grilling the steaks? My dinner began to churn in my stomach as I thought about him watching us. I could not hide my emotions as I began to shake.

The cops advised us to leave town and give Joe a few days to cool off. "Is there any place that you can go that he would not think to look?"

Troy and I decided to drive to his mom's in Sioux City, Iowa, and visit his family. After packing light suitcases, we hit the road while holding hands the entire distance.

Joe was in the military. He is cunning and smart.

Fear overcame me as I played different scenarios over and over in my mind. Troy was steady as a rock, assuring me that we would be okay.

The big question I deliberated on was why had Joe snapped in the first place? He had left me. Had Sherri decided not to leave Greg, causing Joe to face the reality that he had left me for no reason? I knew him well enough to know he didn't like making wrong decisions, especially ones that made him look like an idiot.

We stayed four days with Troy's family and decided it was time to return home. The first thing I did was secure a restraining order against Joe, hoping that a little applied pressure would keep it from happening again. I knew once he had sobered up, he would come to his senses and realize if he wasn't careful, he could ruin his reputation.

What if he comes back? Is he capable of wounding more than my emotions? Did I even know who this man really was?

Tormented by my thoughts, my cozy little home didn't seem safe anymore. My attorney contacted Joe with a bill for the broken windows in the garage. The check arrived shortly thereafter, enclosed in a blank piece of paper.

My attorney also warned me that because the divorce was filed under "irreconcilable differences," it meant both parties agreed to the arrangement. He said if Joe showed up in front of the judge, the divorce would not be granted. His irrational behavior was certainly cause for concern.

Two days before the finalization of the divorce, I received a call from Joe.

"Rhonda, can we have dinner to see if there are any bits or pieces of our relationship that are salvageable?"

I held my breath, trying to decide how to best answer. If I said no, would that cause him to show up at the court preceding? I did not trust this man.

"Ok, Joe. I will meet you at the little restaurant on Shackleford at 6:30."

I packed up a few items that he had left at the house and put them in the backseat of my car. I knew this would be the last chance I would have to return them and I certainly didn't want to give him an excuse to come back to my house.

I walked into the restaurant with my stomach in knots and my head pounding. The twinkle had returned in Joe's eye. I wouldn't let it deceive me this time.

I sat down and he reached for my hand. "Thank you for coming," he said.

"Joe, I'm not sure what you hope to accomplish. You are very confusing." I didn't mention Sherri. I remembered all too well that he had told me not to mess with him and he had proven that I shouldn't.

"Rhonda, I made a mistake. I've had time to think about it. I'm not sure that I want the divorce."

"Without any warning, you packed your bags and left me. Within twenty-four hours, you loaded a truck with your belongings and left. How can I live with the fear of you doing that again? I can't, Joe."

The food arrived and I finished as quickly as possible. I wanted out of that place. His mouth began to twitch and something inside of me told me to be very careful.

He tried to paint a picture of confusion about what was important to him. As he paid the bill, he suggested we get in the car to talk.

****

I crawled behind the wheel of my car, and as he opened the passenger side door, I saw him glance into the backseat. When he saw his belongings, a cloud of darkness descended upon him, scaring me.

"You didn't have any intentions of trying to make this work when you came here. Did you?" he asked.

I froze, unsure of what to do or say. He turned to me with angry, heated eyes and grabbed me by the throat, slamming my face hard against the window. A couple happened to be in the car parked next to me. They watched in horror as I mouthed the words, "Help me. Please." I watched them lower their heads and drive away.

Joe grabbed my leg, ripping my pants.

"Please stop, please stop!" I screamed.

Suddenly, as quickly as this nightmare started, it stopped. He opened the door and slammed it shut. Blood rose to the surface of my leg and my head throbbed. What do I do? I looked in the rearview mirror and watched him drive away. I burst into tears, the relief opening a river of salt upon my cheeks. After gaining my composure I drove home.

What if Joe is outside watching?

I closed all the blinds and made sure all the doors were locked. Then I called Troy to tell him what had happened. He begged me to let him come over. I didn't think that was a good idea, knowing it would fuel Joe's anger. I had the feeling he was a ticking time bomb that could explode at any moment.

I barely slept as the bigger question loomed in my head. What will happen if he shows up at the judge's chamber in two days?

Forty-eight hours later, I dressed for freedom. Landis, my partner, went with me just in case I needed help. I knew Troy should not be in proximity to the courthouse.

Landis and I walked into the large stone building, where we found my attorney waiting. My eyes were darting to and fro, watching intently for Joe. We made it to the courtroom with still no sign of him. My name was called to stand before the judge. He asked if my husband was present and I replied, "He is not, Your Honor."

After a few formalities, the paperwork was signed and once again, I returned to the familiar name of Rhonda Taylor.

I felt relief, yet I realized I now had two failed marriages.

I left the courthouse and drove to meet Troy, who waited to hear whether or not Joe had shown up. As he opened his front door I couldn't help but throw my head back and scream, "It's over!"

He ran to me, throwing his arms around my waist, pulling me close. As we kissed, I felt relief wash over the pain, which had paralyzed my body for some time.

Inside the new home he had recently purchased awaited a fire, wine, cheese, and a small gift wrapped very carefully.

"It looks as though you were anticipating a celebration," I said with a smile.

Troy took my hand and told me he was thrilled that I was no longer married and free to explore a relationship with him. He said, "I have something that I want you to listen to." As the music began to play, he handed me the lyrics to a song by Basia entitled "Time and Tide."

Thirteen

"You will make known to me the path of life…"

Psalm 16:11

Nineteen-eighty-nine rolled in with joy and anticipation for what the new year could bring. I was ready to begin a fresh season of life. The big 3-0 was right around the corner, causing me to reflect on my dreams and aspirations.

As a child, I'd dreamt of having lots of children because I didn't like being an only child. As my biological clock ticked, I realized my dream of motherhood was possibly just that—a dream.

A surprise phone call from Mother made me look deeply within myself once again.

Mother had been attending church with Howard Lee every Sunday since they married. Her call was to tell me she had accepted Jesus into her heart as her Lord and Savior. I could tell she was excited and I knew I should share her elation, but my heart was indifferent.

All I could muster up was, "That's great, Mother. I'm happy for you."

God took Daddy. Would I ever believe otherwise? I knew I needed God, or at least I grew up believing my Mama Dora when she told me I did. *How did she forgive God for taking her son? How do people have faith when life is so hard?* So many questions lingered in my mind. Even though

I had cried out to God to forgive me, then joined the church, I had fallen right back into my old patterns.

God surely is disappointed. I don't want to think about it. He has disappointed me, too.

****

My relationship with Troy moved along nicely until things came to a screeching halt when he was offered a promotion in Detroit, Michigan.

It was obvious he was uncertain of what to do. He said, "This is great for my career, but where does that leave us?"

"Well, absence supposedly makes the heart grow fonder. We can try a long-distance relationship and see what happens or we can end it," I replied.

"Do you want to end it?" he asked.

"No, Troy, I don't. But we have only dated eight months." Surely he understood I was still gun shy of another serious relationship.

We agreed that, regardless of the many miles between us, we were going to give it a shot. He would be moving the first week of July; he asked if I would travel to Michigan with him to help him move into his new home. The company he worked for took care of the sale of his home in Little Rock, and he decided to rent an apartment for a while before making a decision on another purchase.

We arrived in Motor City and took a couple of days to explore before the moving van arrived. The van arrived early on our last day together, giving us the day to unpack. I'd planned a nice dinner and got busy preparing in the kitchen. As the sun went down, I turned on some music and lit a few candles. The ambiance, combined with the aroma of homemade spaghetti sauce, should have been an indication for Troy to stop unpacking and enjoy our last evening together.

I was wrong. Troy continued to unpack, and with the opening of each new box my internal temperature rose another degree. All he could say was, "Just a couple more boxes…"

I snapped. "Are you telling me those boxes are more important than spending time with me? I leave in the morning and we don't know when we will see each other again."

I walked out the door and slammed it as hard as I could. I'm not sure if I was upset about the stupid boxes or if the reality of the many miles between us was already weighing on me. Tears streaming down my face, I went for a brief walk, hoping to give us both a few minutes to clear the air. I returned to find the same scene I had left.

He didn't seem to care. The tears didn't make him stop; he was a man on a mission. I turned the stove off and said, "Fine! Have it your way." I grabbed a blanket and fell asleep on the couch. I awoke early to a hush that filled the air.

My tears resurfaced as we drove to the airport. The silence was deafening. "Don't you have anything to say?" I asked.

"Nope."

I got out of the car without saying a single word. I walked miserably through the airport, and the flight attendant on my plane even asked if someone close to me had died.

"No, my boyfriend and I just ended our relationship," I answered through muffled sobs.

Two long weeks passed without a word from Troy. Then one evening my phone rang.

"Hello."

"Rhonda, it's me," Troy said with an uncertain calm in his voice.

My heart leaped, then sunk, then leaped again. I swallowed hard and tried to sound casual. "Well, hi. How've you been?"

"Look, I just need to tell you something. I recently went out with someone," he stammered.

"What am I supposed to say, Troy?"

"Rhonda, you don't need to say anything. I wanted you to know that when I was with her, all I could think about was you. I now know that you are the one for me. That is if you will have me after the way I acted. Will you forgive me?"

He'd said the words every woman longs to hear, and over the next several minutes we were chatting like two crazy teenagers catching up on the past two weeks we'd been apart.

We made plans for him to fly to Little Rock on Labor Day weekend, and not a day passed when we didn't talk. My heart's fondness for him continued to grow.

****

My work partner, Landis, had recently been promoted to the home office in Kansas City, Missouri. He asked if he and his fiancée could take me out to dinner to celebrate before moving. We decided on the last weekend of August, a week prior to Troy coming home.

Landis told me to be ready by 6:00 p.m. I put on a little black leather skirt and leopard print sweater. My long hair had just the right amount of volume and my black suede heels finished the outfit nicely. I looked in the mirror and laughed, thinking about the looks I'd get if I wore this outfit in Bumpus Mills. Those sweet folks would surely think that I was working the corner of Second Avenue.

I was standing by the door and waiting for Landis to arrive when I noticed a limousine driving slowly down my street. It came to a stop in front of my home. The driver got out and walked up to my door, asking for Landis.

"Sir, you must be mistaken."

"If you are Rhonda, I know for certain that I'm to pick you up and take you to a restaurant called Graffiti's. Landis must be paying for the bill."

I was shocked. "Well, I'm Rhonda, so let's go."

As we approached the restaurant, the maître d' walked to the limo and opened my door, greeting me with a smile.

"Welcome, Miss Taylor."

My goodness, I wasn't sure what to say. There was a line of people streaming from the door, all of them curious as to who had just arrived in the limo. The maître d' took me to a table set for two.

"I'm sorry," I said. "I think there is a mistake. I'm meeting a couple. There should be three seats."

The maître d' didn't seem to listen but proceeded to pull my chair out for me to take a seat. A long-stemmed yellow rose lay before me—my favorite flower. A card with my name on it was lying next to the rose. My heart began to beat rapidly, even though I wasn't sure why. Landis had become a good friend, but these details were over the top. I opened the card and read, "If you would like to have dinner with a very lonely gentleman, look over your shoulder."

I slowly turned around to see Troy walking toward me, dressed to the nines. I jumped out of my chair when I saw the joy written all over his face. As he reached for me, the overcrowded restaurant burst into applause. The noise surrounding us dissolved in the passion of our embrace.

"I can't believe you are here! I thought you were coming next weekend!" I beamed.

I couldn't restrain my tears as we sat down and our salads were placed on the table.

"Troy, I'm not sure I can eat."

"Sweetheart, I have a very special evening planned. Just eat your salad," he replied as he looked down at my plate.

I followed his gaze and noticed my plate was different from his. I glanced into his eyes, searching for an explanation, but he only smiled. I carefully pushed the romaine to the side, exposing words etched in blue on the beautiful ceramic dish.

My dearest Rhonda, my lover, my best friend;
Till eternity with you I will spend.
My wife, I hope you will be,
So, my sweet Rhonda,
Will you marry me?

Troy, staring intently into my eyes, said, "Well? I'm waiting for an answer."

"Yes, Troy! I will!"

He motioned for the headwaiter, who arrived at the table with a bottle of Dom Pérignon Champagne and popped the cork, indicating a reason to celebrate. Strangers around us shared our joy. Love was in the air as Troy's kiss confirmed to the world that I'd said yes.

My childhood dreams for a prince could not have imagined a more perfect proposal.

Until that gnawing feeling returned.

I sure hope the third time is a charm.

I excused myself and made my way to the ladies' room; diners throughout the room congratulated me along the way. I was so excited, yet that old familiar feeling of fear returned. *I will not let anything spoil this night,* I said to myself. I touched up my makeup and returned to the man who would become my third husband.

When we arrived home, I told him I needed to call my mother to give her the news.

"Mother…"

"Hi, Honey. It's awfully late. Why are you calling? Is everything okay?"

It was good to hear her voice, but I was unsure how she would receive my news. I clung to the certainty that nothing would change her love for me.

I said, "Yes, Mother. Troy proposed and we're getting married!" I exclaimed, trembling from both fear and excitement.

She paused, taking in the impact of what I was telling her. "Are you sure?"

"Yes, Mother. I'm sure." *Am I sure? Am I trying to convince Mother or myself?*

No, I'm not sure. I mean, yes—I am sure, but I'm scared. Back and forth my mind raced.

She quickly remarked, "Well, you don't want to shoe the horse all the way around."

That was Mother's way of saying I'd better not have to get married a fourth time. I assured her this was my third and final time to walk down the aisle.

Troy had made plans the following day to visit a jeweler together, as he wanted to make sure that I loved the ring. His thoughtful heart calmed my anxiety.

There was so much to talk about. We continued celebrating over lunch with a glass of wine and an appetizer, and I declared, "I have always wanted a Christmas wedding."

He almost choked on his cheese. He had done a lot of planning to make the proposal special, assuming there would be a long engagement. But as we talked, we both agreed that we didn't want to be apart any longer than necessary.

Little Rock seemed to be the perfect location for our wedding, and Troy determined that he would like to marry in the Catholic Church, which suited me fine. With so many plans and a short amount of time, we headed to a Catholic church he had visited on occasion.

A priest met us and his very first question was, "Have either of you been married before?"

"Yes, sir. I have. Actually, twice."

"Well, the church will be happy to marry you after you go through an annulment process for each divorce."

Troy spoke up. "How long does that take?"

"I'm afraid, son, that it could take quite some time."

I was crushed to have my past interfere with our wedding plans. Troy didn't understand—nor agree—with the position of the church, and he told the priest exactly that.

As we walked out, he said, "Let's go to your church."

Admittedly, I was embarrassed to return to Brother James for a second marriage. And I secretly hoped he didn't keep up with the attendance records.

"Ok, Troy. Let's go there now. Maybe we will be lucky enough to see him."

To my surprise and without any questions, Brother James said he was happy to marry us.

"December second it is."

And just like that, the wedding plans were set in motion.

****

Troy had never been married and wanted the entire kit and caboodle. My first wedding had been traditional, the second private and quaint. If the third time was to be the charm, we would need to make it memorable.

Wearing white did not seem appropriate, so I chose to wear a fitted, dark-cream formal wedding dress laden with pearls and sequins. The neckline scooped low in the front and back, the sleeves long and puffed. I decided I would wear my hair up with a small poof for a veil that accentuated my big hair.

The wedding plans came together quickly, with the festive holiday season providing a backdrop of lights and poinsettias. The bridesmaids would wear tea-length, dark-green skirts and low-cut, velvet black tops with rhinestone buttons. The men decided upon black tuxedos for the formal occasion.

With the wedding plans in order, the focus shifted to the selling of my home. I put a FOR SALE BY OWNER sign in my yard and it only took one open house for it to sell. *How could I be so lucky?* I wondered.

Our good fortune continued as we immediately found a new home in Canton, a city outside of Ann Arbor, Michigan, that was perfect for us. I'd be able to continue my career in the pharmaceutical industry from there. Everything was falling into place nicely, as though it was specially orchestrated.

The wedding drew near and the time came to mail the invitations. I asked Troy about inviting his biological father, Skip. I couldn't understand not wanting to pursue a relationship with his father. I still missed mine deeply.

"Please, Troy, let's invite him," I asked.

Troy gave in and Skip was delighted to receive his invitation. To our surprise, he even offered to pay for the rehearsal dinner. Troy hesitated, but I felt it was Skip's way of trying to make up for his absence in Troy's life.

****

The big weekend arrived, with the rehearsal dinner ushering in the big event. I was a bit shocked when I met Skip for the first time. Troy looked identical to his father, except for the toupee, of course, and even though Troy's brothers were complete opposites, I was smitten with both of them, as well.

On the second of December, with seventy-five of our closest friends and family, Troy and I prepared to take our vows as man and wife.

Troy's mom and grandma seemed overjoyed, as did my mother, even though I'm sure she prayed that this would be the last wedding for her daughter.

For the second time, Howard Lee met me at the back of the church to walk me down the aisle. "Rhonda, are you absolutely sure this time? I don't want to do this again."

I laughed and answered, "Me, either. Let's do it."

I had no hesitation to become Mrs. Troy Madge as I looked down the aisle at the man waiting for me.

"Who gives this woman to wed this man?" Brother James asked.

"Her mother and I," replied Howard Lee.

Troy took my hand and squeezed it tightly. There was a gentle strength in his soft hands. Our eyes met with a glistening that opened the window to our souls as we stood before God to take our vows.

"Troy, you may kiss your bride," Brother James declared after we'd finished our vows.

I could not control the small drip from my nose, which had clung to the tip the entire ceremony, even through the sniffles. I reached to wipe it off before he kissed me, but Troy didn't seem to care. He had accepted me for better or worse. His kiss lingered.

Brother James interrupted, "I now introduce to you Mr. and Mrs. Troy Madge."

I wanted to skip, jump, run, anything, but my tight-fitting dress constricted me. Birdseed flew through the air as we left the church. The little poof in my hair was surely a nice attraction for birds in the area, where food would be plentiful for months to come.

Our limo awaited and drove us to the Little Rock Capitol Hotel for the reception. Food and drink welcomed us into the beautiful old building filled with twinkling lights and smells of the holiday season.

Troy and I were making our way to the dance floor when we heard our song, "Time and Tide." It was hard to contain my happiness as Troy twirled me in his arms. When that song ended, the "Tennessee Waltz" induced laughter from everyone when Troy grabbed Mother and Howard Lee took my arm. Who knew this quiet, subdued man could tear up a dance floor? The split in the back of my dress may have increased in length, but I didn't care.

This night was the beginning of a lifelong journey. The feeling of rest-assured confidence was unfamiliar. It came with knowing I had finally found the one.

Fourteen

"Behold, children are a gift of the Lord, the fruit of the womb is a reward."

Psalm 127:3

Don Ho's song, "Tiny Bubbles in the Wine," was certainly appropriate for our honeymoon in Maui. I had never been to a more beautiful place in my life. In December, poinsettias grow on the side of the road much like wildflowers do in Tennessee during the spring.

Troy and I enjoyed reminiscing about every detail of our wedding and the week in paradise, but life moved on and it was time to get back to work. Double income with no kids opened doors to a full life. However, like most newly married couples, there were bumps in the road.

We had only been married a short time when Troy started to grumble about working for Kirsch, the manufacturer of drapery hardware. He'd grown up with an entrepreneurial heritage, beginning with his grandfather who had opened the drapery store Troy started working at when he was fifteen. Troy decided that he could open an installation business and install blinds and draperies for small companies in the area. Working for himself would not continue the secure income and benefits he was accustomed to, but my career afforded us a safety net, so I encouraged him to do whatever would make him happy.

I soon came to find out the source for Troy's true joy was found in his toolbox.

"Hey, Rhonda, I think I'm going to build a deck."

"Troy, let's just hire someone to do it."

"You don't think I can build it, do you?"

"Well, actually, no."

Those were the wrong words for me to say, but I hadn't grown up with men in my family who were handy. Therefore, I assumed Troy wasn't, either. He was determined to prove me wrong. It was the first time I saw signs of anger in him.

"Are you stressed, Troy? What is wrong?" I asked.

Not realizing it, I opened the floodgates.

"For one thing, you are driving me crazy leaving so many lights on in the house. When I drove up tonight, I sat and counted twelve lights on in different rooms. Why is that necessary? You can't be upstairs and down at the same time," he said with a smirk.

"I like a bright home. I don't like being in the dark," I replied.

"Our electric bill is going to be through the roof. I'm telling you right now to stop it. When you leave a room, turn those lights off. Do you understand?" he yelled.

Blessed be the peacemaker, echoed in my mind. So I said I was sorry and didn't say another word.

The lights issue started to be a daily argument, with the exception of weekends. Fortunately, we had made friends with another newlywed couple, and almost every Friday night we got together with them for a competitive game of cards and good food. Thankfully, the weekend fun overshadowed the arguments from the week.

We shared a lot in common with our new friends Jess and Sam. Sam was another local rep in the pharmaceutical industry. Deep conversations about our life experiences were had over cards, and I decided to open up about my past and told them I'd been married twice before. Jess was shocked. I could tell it didn't settle well with her. She didn't say anything that night, but a couple of weeks later, I stopped by their home after work just to say hello. Jess wasn't home yet, so I sat with Sam in the living room and chatted about the day's work.

Jess walked in and the strangest look came across her face. Sam jumped up to give her a kiss, but her gaze was on me.

"What's wrong? Are you okay?" I asked.

"Well, actually, no. I'm not," she answered. "I don't like coming home to find my husband with a woman who is on her third husband."

"Oh. I'm not sure what to say. I guess that means you don't trust me," I replied.

She didn't have to respond. The look in her eyes said everything. I could feel the expression on my face reflecting the deep hurt she had thrust into my heart. I felt a single tear slide from the corner of my eye. I stood to leave, and neither of them tried to stop me.

The drive home was miserable.

Do all women think the same thing? If so, no one will trust me.

Did Jess think I was coming on to Sam? How could I ever make her believe that I would never do anything with her husband? The haunting thoughts were agonizing.

Troy came home shortly after I returned. I shared what happened and made up my mind right then that I would not tell anyone else about my past. Ever. No one needs to know the truth. The pain of someone else's judgment was unbearable. I refuse to put myself in that situation again.

A couple of weeks passed before we heard from Jess and Sam again. The awkwardness of the first night was strangling. We never mentioned what happened in their home, or my past for that matter. I had hoped she would apologize, but that was wishful thinking on my part. I made a point to never be alone again with Sam.

****

I felt a need to make everyone around me happy, including my husband. I was determined to make my marriage work, although there were days I questioned whether or not I could. My new husband was a controller. He had to have power over every situation, so to make life easier, I relented.

Troy proved he could build by constructing the biggest deck in the neighborhood. I praised him for his work and apologized for doubting him. It seemed I was always the one having to say those words.

After two years of marriage, the fights escalated and the familiar, troublesome thoughts of leaving returned.

How can I live this way?

Why am I the one who always has to say I'm sorry?

I knew without a doubt that if this were my first marriage, I would not stay. I felt trapped, but how could I get a third divorce? If I left him, I'd be faced with either living alone the rest of my life or getting married a fourth time. Mother's words echoed about shoeing the stupid horse all the way around.

I was in a doctor's office one day, making a sales call, and I happened to overhear a conversation about counseling for couples. I really didn't know anything about it but decided to ask Troy what he thought. To my surprise, he told me to find a therapist and he would go with me.

I found a counselor and scheduled our first session, a two-hour appointment. We briefly discussed our background together and why we needed help. I became uncomfortable knowing that unless we were honest with him and each other, we would not receive the help we needed.

I confessed, "I cannot stand living with a man who feels he is always right and has to be in control of every situation."

Troy complained, "Rhonda leaves all the lights on in the house, and regardless of what I say, she doesn't change. She doesn't listen to me."

The counselor began to ask Troy deep questions about his past. Troy revealed many of the stories I had heard before, but this time it was as though I was hearing them for the first time. They talked in detail about his father and being raised by an alcoholic mother who married multiple times in search of happiness.

All of a sudden the counselor said, "Troy, I believe that around the time you entered puberty, you looked at your family and decided that you were not going to be like them. You decided to take control."

I was shocked. I had never thought about that before. Troy could have wandered on the same path as his family, but he didn't; he chose the road less traveled. For the first time, I looked at my man through eyes of respect; the one thing every man desired.

Then Mr. Counselor looked at Troy and said, "Son, I will also tell you that you will add years to your life by reducing your stress if you will simply turn off the lights yourself without saying a word to Rhonda."

I did the happy dance in that man's office. It was the best $100 I had ever spent.

Something significant happened that day. Our level of commitment deepened, and with that came the desire to have a family.

****

We only tried for a couple of months before I was able to announce, "Troy, we are having a baby!"

It was a surreal feeling to know I had a child growing within me. Will it be a boy or girl? What will he or she look like?

What if something is wrong with the baby?

Stop. I chose to not think about anything going wrong. We wanted to tell the world that we were going to be parents. This would be the first grandbaby in both families.

Our joy was short lived. Six weeks later I began to bleed. I screamed, "There's blood!"

Troy came running. He tried to console me as we called the doctor's office. We were told to come in immediately.

An ultrasound confirmed our fears. We left that day with a level of sadness that neither of us had experienced before. We were forced to say good-bye to a precious life we wanted with all our hearts. The doctor tried to encourage us by telling us miscarriages were very common and we would be able to try again after four months.

God could have prevented this.

Death. More death.

Why, God? Couldn't You have done something?

Once again I found myself asking the same questions that I asked when Daddy died. Did I expect an answer this time? We felt so alone in our grief, miles apart from family.

Although we continued to mourn the loss of our child, we did learn from others that miscarriages are common. Somehow, that was helpful and brought hope. Four months later we tried again, and just as quickly as before, I was carrying a child. I was scared to death that I would do something wrong. After all, had it been my fault that I lost my first baby? The doctor assured me that I should go about life as normal.

Two months later, I experienced miscarriage number two.

I grew weary and depressed.

Was God punishing me for the lifestyle I had lived?

People would say how sorry they were for us, but I preferred not to hear anything. "I'm sorry" seemed to always come after losing someone and I couldn't handle hearing those words again.

Troy and I were nestled on the couch when he surprised me with his next words.

"Rhonda, maybe we should go to church. Isn't that where people go when they need help?"

He was asking the wrong person. I wasn't convinced, but I surprised myself by answering, "Sure. Why not?"

****

The following Sunday, we found ourselves in a local church. There were no hymns or memorized rhetoric. Actually, people seemed to really be passionate about being there. We liked it and it made us feel as though we were doing something right.

Another four months passed, and we tried for another baby. Once again the pregnancy test was positive. Our doctor explained that if I should miscarry once again, I was to go straight to an infertility specialist as soon as possible, meaning within the hour of the first sign of blood.

Two months later I had my third miscarriage.

Troy and I called the specialist and we were told to get to the clinic quickly. We'd be given tests to provide answers as to why this was happening. We were both numb by this point and wanted a solution.

The doctor walked in our room and said, "I believe I have found your problem and it's rather simple to fix. You are producing an antibody that attacks the fetus. There is evidence to prove that taking a baby aspirin every day will destroy the antibody and you will be able to carry a baby full term."

"It could really be that easy?" I asked.

He explained that he had seen success many times. "I want you to start taking a baby aspirin today, but you need to wait the four-month period again before trying to get pregnant to allow your body a chance to recover."

Time passed and I became pregnant for the fourth time. I took the aspirin each morning as prescribed. Eight weeks passed. Then ten weeks, then twelve.

Petrified, we went in for an ultrasound. What if we have gotten our hopes up for nothing? The ultrasound nurse started the search as she pressed my stomach. Suddenly, I heard an unfamiliar sound, the most beautiful my ears had ever heard—the heartbeat of our baby.

"Oh, Troy..."

Our dreams were coming true. We were having a baby. We called our parents to share the news. Mother had been a rock through this whole ordeal and I missed her terribly. I wanted to be close to her again as the journey of parenthood was about to begin. We began to wonder if we'd want to raise a child in Michigan so far away from family.

Not only that, but I missed living in the South. The month of April brought dogwood blossoms in the hills of Tennessee, while dirty snow piles lingered on our streets in Canton, Michigan. I wanted to move home and raise our baby as a Southerner.

After a little research, I found out there was an opening with my company in Chattanooga, Tennessee, only four hours from Mother and Howard Lee. The company said they were willing to relocate me, and since Troy had established his own business, he could easily move.

We had not a single doubt that we wanted to move from the frozen tundra back to Rocky Top. With our minds set and our bags packed, we moved to a sweet, little lakeside house in Soddy Daisy, a small town just outside of Chattanooga.

We quickly settled into life in this picturesque community. Thankfully my new sales territory was small, which meant after I had the baby, I could pick up our little one every day at a decent hour. Troy's reputation as an installer presented him with work the very first week.

I really couldn't believe our luck and how everything fell into place, just like it did when we left Little Rock. I never thought of myself as lucky, but maybe I was. What else could have caused our lives to come together so nicely?

Our favorite time came when we went to bed at night. There was such tenderness in the stroke of Troy's hand over my stomach, followed by the wonder and excitement as we watched the baby kick and turn.

"Wow, it says that childbirth is the worse pain known to mankind," Troy announced one evening while reading a pregnancy book.

"And why on earth would you choose to read that to me?"

He laughed. "Don't worry. It will be worth it."

I really had not thought about the pain. I just couldn't wait to find out if the baby was a boy or a girl. We decided to wait until the delivery to find out since life doesn't offer many opportunities to be really surprised. This would be one.

One month before my due date, our doctor announced that the baby was breach and scheduled a Cesarean section.

The date was set for the third of September. Both mothers came to Soddy Daisy the day before to have dinner and go to the hospital together.

I worked hard in the house most of the day to prepare for our baby's arrival. With dinner on the stove and excitement bubbling over, I realized my back hurt. This was followed by a contraction.

"Troy, I think you should call the doctor."

As he hung up the phone, he said we had to get to the hospital quickly. No chances could be taken with a breach baby.

One thing about Troy is that he follows the law, even with his wife having contractions in the front seat next to him. I told him to get me to the hospital and forget about the speed limit. The moms were in the backseat, holding on for dear life when suddenly a cop pulled out behind us from a side road. Troy's mom rolled down her window and flung her body halfway out, screaming, "We are having a baby!"

Troy pulled over as the officer jumped out of his car. Troy explained the situation. "Officer, will you put her in your car?"

Being the kind Southern gentleman that he was, he replied, "Sir, I will not."

He called for an ambulance, which happened to be just blocks away. I was quickly on my way to the hospital while the EMT examined me. I heard him say to the doctor on the phone, "She is 100 percent effaced and dilated to seven centimeters." They started an IV and hit the gas with three crazies following behind.

During all the excitement, Troy realized he had forgotten a VHS tape for our recorder so he sent his mom to find one. After she found a tape at the market, she rushed to find where Troy was waiting but somehow became disoriented in the hospital and walked out a door that led into a garden. When the door shut, it immediately locked her out. Her only way back into the interior corridor of the hospital was to climb a garden trellis and enter through a window on the next floor up. Determined not to miss her grandbaby's birth, she threw her purse over her shoulder and started climbing, making it just in time.

As I was quickly prepared for surgery, Troy stood by my head with the nurse. A sheet had been draped so that I could not see, but Troy had a bird's-eye view. Within minutes, I heard the words, "It's a girl!"

On September 2, 1993, Taylor Rae Madge was born—all seven pounds and thirteen ounces of beautiful, with creamy, olive skin and dark hair just like her daddy.

As the doctor handed her to Troy for the first time, I heard him gasp. He brought her close for me to see. It was killing me not to hold her.

"Oh, Troy, look at her hair and her little feet."

When they brought her to me in my recovery room and laid her in my arms to nurse, I knew that I was experiencing indescribable joy.

"Hi, my sweet Taylor. I'm your mother." I drew her next to me as the softness of her skin met mine. Her eyes looked up to me as her tiny mouth found my breast, just the way God intended.

God? The stream of tears fell from my eyes as I looked at my baby. I knew in that moment that there had to be a God who loved me to have given me such a gift. For the first time, instead of questioning God, I turned my eyes toward heaven with a grateful heart and whispered, "Thank You."

FIFTEEN

"I know the plans that I have for you declares the Lord..."

Jeremiah 29:11

M otherhood was everything I had dreamed it would be. Every day seemed to bring another new experience, and I obsessed over doing everything perfectly for Taylor. On the morning of her first checkup, I cried the entire drive, knowing for sure I had done something wrong to her in her young life. When the doctor looked at me and said, "Well done, Mama. She looks great," I threw my arms around his neck and gave him a big hug.

My eight weeks of maternity leave flew by quickly. My heart ached at the thought of leaving our little angel with anyone, but we found a dear lady to care for her, which made it a tad easier to return back to work.

Martha Hudson became Mamaw to our family. She was one of those kind, older women who exuded warmth with her smile, bright eyes, and welcoming spirit. She was a true gift who walked into our lives at the perfect time, a woman who loved well and gave of herself selflessly. Mamaw had a small group of children she watched in her home, and she loved each one as if they were her own.

Mamaw also wanted everyone to know that she loved Jesus. "You guys have to get this baby into a church," she boldly told us.

Since moving back down south, life had seemed a lot smoother, so we hadn't felt the need for church. After all, we didn't have any fires to put out, and that was the only reason I had ever found to go to church. However, becoming parents to Taylor caused us to look at church with a different perspective because we wanted what was best for her.

The following Sunday, we visited a small church near our home. Pastor Steve welcomed our family with open arms. Of course, he didn't know all my secrets—and I didn't intend to tell him, either. But to step back into the house of God without feelings of desperation was quite different.

Troy and I sat on a pew with Taylor asleep in my arms. I felt a familiar stirring in my heart that I hadn't felt for years. I knew our little family was right where we were supposed to be.

****

According to my life's pattern, at least until this point, most of my happiest moments had been short-lived. Not in a glass-half-empty way; it just so happened that my sweet moments came and went swiftly, and I accepted that as my reality. Right now, things in the Madge household were great. Taylor brought sweet laughter and elation into our lives and we loved being parents. So when our wondrous moments took a downhill turn, I wasn't really surprised.

"Rhonda, I really need to talk to you."

I heard the seriousness in Troy's words.

As Taylor slept, I listened to Troy express his unhappiness in his business. "I'm just going through the motions every day. I'm not being challenged anymore and I'm bored." He told me he wanted to look for something else to do, but he was unsure of what that could possibly be.

Two days later, Troy walked in and said, "Pack a bag. We are taking a little trip to New York."

"New York? Why on earth would we go there?"

"Well, I have been researching this new business opportunity. Actually, it's a franchise called the Treasure Cache. It's a type of retail store and it sounds really promising."

Troy explained that a broker had presented the concept to him and had assured him that it was a no-fail opportunity. The Treasure Cache was a store that rented shelf space to artisans and crafters so they could sell their merchandise in a high-traffic mall setting.

"Troy, you seem really excited. I want you to be happy, Sweetheart. It almost sounds too good to be true, though."

Still, a week later we traveled to New York. We learned there were twenty-one other stores, primarily in the northeast. The owners were excited to expand into Tennessee because the South is known for their quality craftsmanship.

We were exhilarated on our flight home as we talked through the possibilities. However, once we returned home and settled in, the *what-ifs* began to creep in.

"What if it fails? What if we lose everything?" Troy asked.

"Well, Mother always told me that a couple could live in a pup tent as long as they had love."

"Rhonda, you haven't ever lived in a pup tent."

"No, I haven't. But I know that I love you and I want more than anything for you to be fulfilled as a man."

The next day, the paperwork was signed. We became owners of a store in the Chattanooga mall.

The following days were a pattern of movement that began with an early alarm. I loved the mornings with Taylor and I tried to stretch out the moments as long as possible. But twelve-hour days at the mall for Troy meant everything at home was left up to me, even with a full-time career.

The store opening was successful, and although Troy was working long days, he seemed rewarded. But there was something on my mind.

I was thirty-five years old and I wanted another child. I knew if we waited much longer, it might not happen. I did not want Taylor to grow up as an only child like I did; it was too lonely a childhood. *What if I miscarried again?* Maybe I should start taking baby aspirin again, just in case.

"Troy, can we please have another baby? I know the timing isn't perfect, but is there ever a perfect time?"

On Valentine's Day 1995, Austin Lee Madge was born, weighing in at seven pounds and thirteen ounces. He was blonde, with a fair complexion and cobalt-blue eyes, the exact opposite of Taylor.

My delivery was normal this time, but because the doctor was going out of town, he wanted to induce my labor. Strangely enough, we were asked to be at the hospital at midnight to begin the process and break my water. On our way, Troy needed to stop at Kinko's to make copies of payroll for employees. I decided to get out of the car and join him, not realizing the keys were locked inside.

Once again, his mom came to our rescue and brought an extra set of keys. My mother was at home with Taylor, waiting for us to call and announce our baby's birth. Once again we waited to be surprised.

Taylor was seventeen months old when she met Austin Lee for the first time. Mother brought her into the hospital room and she crawled upon the bed with me to take a peek at her new brother. "Nose?" she asked. "Eyes?"

"Yes, Taylor. He is just perfect. Don't you think?"

She wrinkled her nose and fell back, laughing. He was perfect and I knew Troy thought so, too. Troy climbed into bed with me and the four of us snuggled together. This is what I had dreamed of my entire life.

Soon everyone left the hospital room, leaving Austin and I to become acquainted as mother and son. I looked deeply into his blue eyes and sang the little song I had learned in Sunday school. *"Jesus loves me this I know, for the Bible tells me so, little one to Him belongs, they are weak, but He is strong."* Once again, I knew we had been given a gift.

Having Little Miss Priss as a toddler along with a newborn made for a tired mama. I couldn't even go to the bathroom alone. Taylor fired questions at me all day about her little brother. I'm pretty sure she thought he was her baby. Whenever he grunted, cried, or smiled, her favorite thing to say was, "It's okay. It's okay."

Life with two babies and a new business felt like we were living in a pressure cooker. To make matters worse, I knew I had to go back to work in a couple of weeks as my maternity leave was coming to an end.

The Chattanooga store grew extremely fast. It was fun to go in and see what new items the artisans had brought in. One Saturday during the Easter holiday rush, I took the babies to surprise their daddy. I had Austin in a front pack and Taylor in a stroller. As we entered the store, Taylor screamed, "Daddy!" After becoming unbuckled, she jumped in his arms, expecting a tour of all the pretty items on the shelves.

A stream of customers came and went as our employees took care of their needs. Taylor said, "Down, Daddy," so she could take a closer look at a baby doll.

I said, "Taylor, you stay close to Daddy, okay?"

That same moment, a customer asked Troy a question. I had my eye on Miss Priss as she chatted away at the pretty doll. In the quick moment when I turned to Austin to adjust his pacifier and looked back down, Taylor was gone.

The store was small. It only took moments to examine the area. Then my eye caught a man running with Taylor by his side out the door into the mall traffic. I screamed and ran toward him, trying to balance Austin in my arms.

"Stop him! Stop him! He has my baby!"

Every person in the store froze.

The strange man stopped and turned toward me. "Is she your daughter, ma'am?"

"What are you doing?" I yelled at him. "Of course, she is mine!"

I grabbed Taylor, who didn't even understand what had happened. People gathered around us as the poor man explained that he had thought another woman had left the store without her daughter. He was chasing someone else in hopes of being the Good Samaritan, not realizing Taylor was mine.

It took hours for my heart to beat correctly. Troy tried to console me, but I couldn't stop crying. The fear of losing my baby was more than I could comprehend. All the while, Austin slept soundly, nestled close to my chest.

Within just six months, the Treasure Cache was making a profit. Troy was ecstatic and thought we should go ahead and open another store, possibly in Nashville.

"Troy, I don't know. Will you travel back and forth? We would not see you very much."

"Didn't you recently find out the Nashville territory is available with your company?" he asked.

"Yeah. What are you thinking, Troy?"

"I have a great manager for the store here, Rhonda. What if your company transferred you to Nashville and we moved there? We would also be closer to your mother and Howard Lee." He continued, excitedly. "Rhonda, if we have two stores making this kind of money, you can quit in a couple of years."

I did like the sound of quitting my job and also being closer to Mother, so I agreed to check into it.

I'm not certain how things happened so quickly, but the pharmaceutical company I worked for seemed thrilled with the idea. Nashville had the worse sales in the entire United States for the drug I was currently selling. I had a proven track record of success and they were eager to place a seasoned representative into the Nashville market, which had much greater potential than Chattanooga.

Within a matter of weeks the relocation was set in motion and Troy prepared to open our second store.

Moving again came easy for us. Within days we were preparing to move just outside of Nashville into a historical community called Franklin.

We were excited for many reasons; however, unbeknownst to us, this is where God had chosen for real transformation to occur.

SIXTEEN

"My sheep hear My voice, and I know them, and they follow Me."

John 10:27

Change. It can bring about a sense of renewal, but it can also result in misery. As I stood on the porch of our home in Soddy Daisy, half-packed boxes at my feet to the left and a baby walker on the floor to my right, I realized how contented I was. When I went back inside the house, I could hear the familiar sounds from the baby monitor as Taylor and Austin woke from their morning naps. This was the home that gave birth to my two greatest joys. Was I really prepared to leave?

I didn't share my confusion or worry with Troy, but continued with the mission of packing all our belongings. As the finishing touches were made to prepare our home for the new owner and load the last box, I thought about our sweet little church and precious Mamaw we were leaving behind.

It was not easy to say good-bye to places that had offered love and acceptance. Of course, they didn't know the truth about me, either. If so, I probably would not have been accepted. I continued to live a façade, fearing my past would cause someone not to trust me. I still lived with the pain of when Jess told me she didn't trust leaving her husband alone with a woman who had been married twice before.

However, with each move it seemed I could leave pieces of my past behind and move forward with the charade, all the while adding another layer of thick skin to insure I wouldn't get hurt again.

****

We pulled up to our newly built brick home located on a cul-de-sac on the east side of Franklin. It had a great yard in the back for the kids to play in and ample room inside for our family of four. We quickly unpacked and settled in because Troy needed most of our time and efforts spent on opening the second store.

We were thankful to have quickly found a woman just like Mamaw to care for Taylor and Austin. Although Miss Dana was much younger than Mamaw, she opened her arms with just the same love for our two babies.

We also continued to take our children to church every Sunday. Regular attendance every week brought assurance that we were doing the right thing. We found a traditional, medium-sized place of worship. I say medium because in this area, there are massive buildings that fill up on Sunday mornings. This was, of course, the center of what is known as the Bible Belt.

Once again, we hit the ground running. Troy established the new store in the local mall and I became acquainted with all the new doctors in my territory.

****

Not long after, I noticed Troy becoming distant and edgy. I knew he was having trouble finding artisans who would sell their merchandise in this new store. If we didn't have enough crafters to support our efforts, we would be unable to pay the rent, which happened to be double what we were paying in Chattanooga.

We had only been open three months when we had to borrow money to keep things afloat. This dream was quickly turning into a nightmare.

I found him crying in the bedroom. "What have I done, Rhonda? We should not have moved here. I have made a terrible mistake."

I didn't want to show my concern, so I tried to encourage him with possible solutions. Mentally, though, he already considered himself a failure.

We couldn't pay the rent the following month and we were going further and further in debt. Troy made the agonizing decision to close both of the stores and file bankruptcy.

"Rhonda, we don't have a choice; they will come after us personally and we could lose our home."

Only four months after opening the second store Troy enlisted the help of an attorney to help us through this terrible process. He told us that both malls could attempt to confiscate any unsold inventory in hopes of recouping their loss. Troy and I made a plan that he would travel to Chattanooga while I stayed at the Franklin store. We simultaneously called all of our vendors and asked them to quietly and quickly come within the hour to retrieve their merchandise without alerting the mall as to what was happening.

The artisans showed up at the stores to claim their things; many of them were nice and understanding, and others were upset and angry.

If an item had sold, we were unable to pay the money owed. One guy in Nashville, who was rather rough around the edges, threatened me. "I will find out where you live," he said angrily. "I don't care if it's the last thing I do, I will get my money back."

I called Troy, scared to death, which completely put him over the edge. His sobs were deafening in my ear.

"What have I done? What have I done? I'm so sorry, Rhonda, to put you through this."

"You listen to me, Troy. We will make it. Do you hear me?"

I didn't know where my strength was coming from because I, too, was terrified of what the future held for us. I could hear my mother telling me that love never fails. But on the other hand, I couldn't imagine how we could possibly recover from our plight.

Troy made it back home that night after we'd finished cleaning out both stores. We laid together in the early morning hours, trying to comfort one another without saying a word. We arose early to spend time with Taylor and Austin. Being with them helped us escape for a while and live in their world filled with cowboys and princesses. With the Treasure Cache doors closed and paperwork filed, we waited to hear from our attorney.

We tried to keep things as normal as possible even though waiting for a judge to make a decision regarding our future was torture. Our refrigerator stopped working in the midst of all of this chaos. Troy went and purchased one of the small ones intended for a dorm room. What a despairing sight it was when Troy placed it in the large space where the former one had set. Taylor thought it was perfect because it was just her size, but when it didn't keep their milk cold, she didn't like it anymore. A couple of weeks passed and I continued to sell drugs and pretend to the outside world that everything was fine. No one knew anything about our troubles except our parents. Finally, the day came to appear before the judge.

Bankruptcy is a peculiar thing. One day you are covered in debt, not sure what the next will bring; then the next day, you don't owe anyone a penny. Thankfully, the bank didn't take our home because there was not enough equity in it to recoup any of their losses, nor were my wages garnished, which allowed us the ability to move forward.

Financially we were going to be okay, but emotionally life began taking a toll. Troy went back to installing window coverings, but he was filled with disappointment and stress. He felt he was a failure to the children and to me. My words didn't seem to bring him comfort.

If it had not been for our neighbors, we would not have pulled through as easily. Several of our yards connected in the back and we routinely gathered to let the kids play while the adults had a cold beverage.

There was one couple in the group, however, who we all called the "Holy Rollers." Their real names were Mell and Julie, but they earned their nickname by going to church two or three nights per week, plus a half day on Sunday. *Why is it necessary to go to church that often?* I questioned.

****

The following Saturday morning, Troy and I were hanging out with the kids in the playroom upstairs. While enjoying what I thought was some great family time, Troy got up and went down to the kitchen. Something told me he needed to be alone.

Time passed slowly before I heard the familiar sound of the backdoor. Taylor Rae and Austin Lee were right in the middle of making Mama look beautiful with a new hairdo, so I couldn't get up to see where Troy had gone.

When I heard my man return, I told my babies to play for a bit by themselves while Mama talked to their daddy alone. As I walked down the stairs, our eyes met, his misty and mine concerned.

"Where have you been, Honey?" I asked.

He sat down at the kitchen table with his head in his hands.

"Rhonda, the thoughts going through my head have been agonizing. I have not been a good husband. It's because of me that we are in the situation we are in. You deserve better."

I sat motionless.

"I was sitting here actually contemplating how to kill myself. Then something strange happened, Rhonda. I don't know if you will believe me or not, but I heard God speak to me. It was not an audible voice. I just heard it in my head."

"What did He say?"

"He told me, 'This isn't what I have for you, Troy.'" The tears fell from his eyes, forming a puddle on the table. "Rhonda, I got up and went next door to Mell and Julie's house, you know, the Holy Rollers. Julie opened the door and I asked her, 'Will you please teach me the Bible?'"

SEVENTEEN

"For I am convinced that neither death, nor life, nor angels, nor principalities, nor things present, nor things to come, nor powers, nor height, nor depth, nor any other created thing, will be able to separate us from the love of God."

Romans 8:38–39

T hat was the moment when things began to change. Hearing God's voice caused Troy to choose another path—the one less traveled.

I later found out that Julie almost jumped into Troy's arms with excitement, all five feet and four inches of her bubbly self. I had never met anyone so joyful. She was close to giggles every time I talked to her.

Mel was much more subdued, with a dry wit Troy and I both appreciated. We soon learned Mell and Julie had loved the Lord their entire lives and had met at a Christian university, which lead to marriage.

They decided to start a Bible study in our home after two other couples also agreed to join us. Evidently, this was a cul-de-sac that knew very little about the Bible or the Creator, for that matter.

The first night the eight of us gathered was rather awkward. Mell asked us what we would like to study. One of the gals spoke up and said, "I've always wanted to know, who were the Jews?"

Mel smiled and said, "We will start with Genesis chapter one."

And that is exactly what we did. We met weekly and studied stories from the Bible. This sweet couple taught from their hearts, never once judging us for our lack of knowledge.

As the weeks passed we grew hungry to know about the unspeakable joy Mell and Julie talked about. We were beginning to look like Holy Rollers ourselves, going to church on Sunday and Wednesday nights, and having Bible study with our neighbors, too.

Troy and I desperately wanted to understand what they meant by "having a relationship" with Jesus. Questions were rampant within our little group. *How is it possible to have a personal relationship with God? How can you communicate with someone who's not here? Can everyone hear God's voice?*

Mel and Julie leaned on the Bible to answer our questions through the experiences of others before us. Lost in my thoughts, I heard Mell say, "The Lord promises that He will never leave you or forsake you."

Wait. I said, "Are you saying through all the beautiful and ugly moments of my life, the Creator of the world has been by my side?" A secure feeling came over me, confirming God was right there with me.

Julie obviously sensed that something was stirring within me. "Rhonda, God loves you because He created you. Why would He abandon His creation?"

"Are you saying that God has stayed with me because He loves me even when I don't deserve it?" I asked.

Julie answered, "Rhonda, that's grace."

That was the most beautiful picture of love I could imagine. "So this relationship you are talking about—is my love returned to God?"

Mel said, "Yes. When you love someone, don't you want them to love you in return?"

It clicked. I realized that because I loved Him so much, I would want to express that love through acts of service, and not because God required me to, but because I would *want* to, simply out of love.

"There is no complex riddle or system of rules that you have to follow in order to be called a Christ-follower. Love covers a multitude of sins," Mell added.

This truth alone sparked a yearning that began an incredible transformation within me. Troy and I went to bed with peaceful hearts as we learned more about this love that God offers. His next words, however, surprised me.

"Rhonda, I'm ready to go to the next step with the Lord."

"We just did. What are you talking about, Honey? As long as I don't have to tell the truth about my past." The peace slipped away as anxiety took over every nook and cranny of my mind. What could possibly be the next step he wanted to take? *He wants me to tell everyone about my past. What would Mell and Julie think of me? If the truth came out, then all of our friends would think I had been dishonest with them all of this time.*

That was my biggest fear—revealing the real me. The woman who was on her third marriage and had done unspeakable things, how could I ever let anyone know that person? If coming clean was the next step, I wanted no part of it.

I rolled over, indicating I was finished with the conversation. How was it possible I had experienced exhilaration unlike anything I could explain just a few hours ago and now be so confused? For the first time in my life, I knew God loved me. How could that feeling vanish so quickly? I whispered, "Lord, please help me to understand."

****

Spring of 1999 marked our fourth anniversary in Franklin. The calendar flipped another year, adding an additional notch to the growth chart for our babies. Taylor loved school and Austin couldn't wait to ride the bus with his sissy. She usually came home each day with a big story to tell her little brother, adding to his agony that he wasn't old enough to share her experiences. She nearly caused me to choke on my chicken one night over dinner when she asked, "Can we adopt?"

Troy and I chimed in at the same moment, "No!"

"Well, why not?" she asked.

We began the song and dance that we were too old and we had two healthy children; there wasn't any reason to adopt.

Taylor said, "But I have a new friend from Russia who was just adopted and I could have a sister just like her."

I later found out about the little girl recently adopted in the first-grade class, and Taylor had been asked to be her room buddy. To our surprise, the little girl lived in our neighborhood, too. The two girls became inseparable. However, we nipped the notion of adoption quickly.

Not long after this I was driving home with the windows down, lost in my thoughts, when I noticed a new subdivision. For some strange reason I decided to pull in and check things out. The model home was lovely. What could it hurt just to walk around? I probably shouldn't have, though, because it caused my mind to reel with ideas. And my excitement didn't wane in the five-minute drive home.

Troy was standing in our kitchen, tired after a long day of work, when I came bursting through the front door with news of my fantastic discovery.

"Troy, you have got to come see the house I found. I mean, it is so spacious and the kids would just love it. It's perfect!" I exclaimed.

"What in the world are you talking about? We aren't looking for a new house, Rhonda. Besides, we couldn't even get financing three years after filing bankruptcy." He walked out of the room.

I thought to myself that I could change his mind if I could just get him there.

The following Sunday after church, when we were all in such good moods, I decided it was the perfect time to bring up looking at the new house. "Hey, Honey, let's drive over and look at that new subdivision I told you about."

"Well, I guess it wouldn't hurt just to look," he said. Of course, Taylor and Austin chimed in, asking questions as to why we would go to see a new house.

Everyone was hooked the second our family walked into that model home.

The builder encouraged us to apply, just to see if we qualified for the loan even though we had filed bankruptcy. Taylor and Austin's pleas pressed on Troy's heart and he agreed to try.

We were approved, much to our surprise, so we decided to see if our house would sell. The FOR SALE sign went up and the house sold within four weeks. I wasn't sure why, but I kept feeling as though we were going to need the additional space.

Once again we packed our bags. It was going to be hard to move from our little cul-de-sac, even though we were just a hop, skip, and a jump away. I was going to miss our neighbors, especially the backyard parties. I also realized we were leaving the home where God had entered our minds and hearts for the first time. Memories that would not soon be forgotten.

****

Our new house was exciting, but the changes happening within the walls was what I loved most. I learned how to pray. Up until this point, I never prayed in front of anyone, not even Troy. Of course, I had prayed with Taylor and Austin: "Now I lay me down to sleep, I pray the Lord my soul to keep. If I should die before I wake, I pray the Lord my soul to take."

I was afraid I would say something wrong in front of others. For some reason, I believed that my prayers needed to impress people instead of just talking with God. Matthew 6:6 spoke to me: "But you, when you pray, go in your inner room, close your door and pray to your Father who is in secret, and your Father who sees what is done in secret will reward you." So that's what I did—I headed to the closet.

Troy and I were both changing, but it still seemed something was missing. The following Sunday, right in the middle of the sermon, he leaned over to me and whispered, "Take a look around. What do you see?"

I glanced around the small sanctuary, and to my surprise half of the congregation was asleep.

I looked over at Troy as he whispered out of the corner of his mouth, "There has got to be a place this doesn't happen."

What Troy meant specifically was that perhaps it was time to find a new church.

The following week he decided to visit a new church by himself. We didn't want to disturb the regular routine for the kids until we determined whether or not we were moving.

The kids and I got home before Troy. He walked in, fired up. "Honey, the message and the music were unbelievable. Let's all go there together next Sunday."

"Well, of course, if that's what you want to do. Let's go," I replied. I wanted to share his excitement.

The week flew by as I anticipated visiting this church Troy had been so ecstatic about. Sunday finally came, and we walked into the largest church I had ever visited and I was not the least bit comfortable.

We walked into the lobby where we were greeted by friendly faces and firm handshakes. I noticed on the wall a plaque displaying the mission statement. It read, "Our mission is to turn ordinary people into passionate followers of Jesus Christ." *Well, we might be at the right place*, I thought. *We are certainly ordinary.*

We found our way into the sanctuary, but there were no pews. On the stage, a band was tuning up. I gently pulled on Troy's sleeve as we found our seats.

"They must not be having their regular service today, Troy. We should probably come back next week."

"No, please. You're going to love it. I promise," Troy whispered back confidently.

We took our seats and the music began. It wasn't hymns; it was more like a rock concert with people clapping and lights flashing. Taylor and Austin joined in, as did Troy. Out of the corner of my eye, it became apparent that I was the only stick in the mud present.

This isn't for me. I don't like it. People aren't dressed up. I don't know the songs.

As soon as the music ended, Pastor Rick White began speaking. His voice was filled with passion, causing me to sit up. I had never heard anyone take scripture and make it so applicable to my life before. I could understand Troy's eagerness to bring us here.

We were sitting in the middle section, and to our right were about four hundred teenagers who had just returned from a camp. I got a tad distracted when I noticed how attentively they were listening to the message.

This is where I want Taylor and Austin.

I turned around, unsure of what just happened, only to realize the same voice that had spoken to Troy at our kitchen table was telling me this was the place He wanted our children to attend church.

Walking out, Troy didn't have to ask if I liked it. With inexpressible joy, I told him what had happened. I wanted to dance, sing, or do something. What else does one do after God speaks to them?

EIGHTEEN

"And you will know the truth, and the truth will make you free."

John 8:32

Our new church was much like a vast ocean, and our family fearlessly jumped right in. At first it was difficult to meet people, but as time went on we began to build friendships. Taylor and Austin adjusted quickly, which made it easier for us, too.

The contemporary music started to speak to me. I was pleasantly surprised when I realized there was a radio station that played many of the same songs I heard on Sunday mornings. I found that helped me during the week to soak in the positive words instead of the songs from my past, which oftentimes made me think about things I wanted to forget.

The Lord was definitely doing something within our family and within me. I found myself in the closet more and more, crying out to God and pleading for forgiveness. I just felt I needed assurance. I knew the Bible said if I asked God to forgive me, He would. However, I was still pretending to be someone I wasn't. I didn't know what the Bible said about that.

Sundays couldn't come soon enough. We were like sponges soaking up everything we could about Jesus. Arriving early allowed us time to wander around some of the booths displayed in the lobby. Troy seemed to linger at one table for quite a while.

"Rhonda, I think I'm going to Guatemala. It's only for seven days and there is a whole missions team going."

I was shocked. I don't think I heard anything Pastor Rick said that day. I sat in my seat convincing myself that he should not go. *Missionaries get killed. I'm going to lose Troy, too. Taylor and Austin won't have a father, just like me.*

The fear of death returned.

We got in the car and I pleaded with him to change his mind.

"Rhonda, I am going to get to build houses. You know how much I love to use my hands. Could God possibly be revealing how He could use me?"

I knew I couldn't say no, and even if I did, he wouldn't listen. Troy had made up his mind that he was going. And he did.

I cried off and on for seven days. I informed every human being I came in contact with that week that *my* husband was on a missions trip in Guatemala, as though he were the only man in history to ever go on such an endeavor.

The kids and I drove to the airport to greet the team on their return. We ran to meet him. Did he look different? Something had changed.

Dinner was waiting in the oven when we got home. We gathered around the dinner table as he recounted story after story of how God had worked there.

"We were pouring a concrete roof one day. There were several of us doing the job because as the concrete was poured, we had to spread it quickly. All of a sudden, a wall of rain moved in our direction. Lightning strikes lit up the sky, followed by bursts of thunder. We knew our roof would be destroyed if it were rained on. One of the men yelled, 'We have to pray!' and we all went to our knees upon that roof."

Troy began to shake and tears fell from his eyes as he recalled what had happened next. "When we finished praying and looked toward the sky, the darkness began to dissipate. It did not rain one single drop on our roof. I witnessed the hand of God."

Taylor, Austin, and I sat speechless—only for a minute, though.

"Tell us more, Daddy! Tell us more!"

Oh, my goodness, what if I had prevented him from going? I thought to myself. I sat and looked at my husband with new eyes. I knew I loved him, but never more than in that moment. My man now knew what it felt like to be the hands and feet of Jesus.

A seed was planted in Troy's heart that trip. It took root and blossomed. He traveled back to Guatemala two more times that year alone, always returning with God-sized stories to be shared.

He also began to change as a man; he seemed more alive every time he returned from a trip. Before he would even unpack, he was already talking about the next one. Taylor and Austin began to get excited about his trips, too, as if little seeds had been planted inside each of them.

Troy begged me to go with him. My reply was always the same: "God provided me with a career and bonuses to pay for these trips. You're meant to go. Not me."

But as God would have it, He had plans for me, also.

****

Large churches really have a hard time, generally speaking, getting people connected. One of the pastors I had become acquainted with asked if I would like to join a committee to start a campaign for small groups. I was interested; it sounded very similar to the little group that had met in our home for two years.

There were six of us on the team that tried to organize the easiest way to form small gatherings of people from the church within their own subdivisions. We spent quite a bit of time together, which led to personal questions.

They are going to ask me about my past. What do I say? Do I tell the truth? I can't lie in church.

"Rhonda, tell us your story. Where did you grow up?"

My bottom lip started to quiver and it became obvious that I was nervous.

The pastor spoke up. "It's okay. Is there something you need to talk about? You are in a safe place."

Really? I know what it feels like to be judged. It hurts. I can't do it. I know they will dismiss me from the committee, too.

Tears. I couldn't stop the flow. And so it happened.

I told my story. I didn't leave anything out, and to my surprise they embraced me. And I was flabbergasted when they said my story needed to be told to others.

"You are kidding, right? You have to realize I have lived a lie the majority of my life. Now you are telling me I should tell others?"

They explained people needed to understand the church is full of hurting people. They felt my story would illustrate the need of not only redemption, but teach what it means to trust others, as well. Ideas began to flow and it was suggested that on kickoff Sunday for small groups, I would share my testimony in front of the entire church.

I didn't know what to say.

After I got home, I went straight to the closet.

The kids don't know the truth. What are they going to say when they find out about their mother?

Lord, what do I do? I'm scared to tell Taylor and Austin the truth, and how in the world am I going to stand before thousands and do the same?

****

Throughout my life I had often heard the saying, "The Lord works in mysterious ways." I was beginning to understand the meaning, which slowly but surely was also mysteriously teaching me how to trust.

It began when we walked into church the following Sunday and Pastor Rick preached on a passage from John 4 about a woman at a well. The story unfolded about a Samaritan woman who met Jesus by a well when she went to draw water. It was a beautiful passage about the living water He could offer her. My heart quivered as Pastor Rick revealed this dear woman had been divorced five times and was currently living with a man. She had more husbands than me. *Is that really in the Bible?* I questioned.

He continued to read from verse 39, saying, "Many of the Samaritans from that town believed in Him because of the woman's testimony: 'He told me everything I ever did.'"

It didn't matter what this woman from the well had done. Jesus used her to tell others about Himself. I knew He was about to use me, too. This was the day the Word of God became personal.

We went home after lunch and I whispered to Troy that I was going to talk to each of the children individually. It had never once dawned on me that I would have to one day sit with my children and tell them about their own mama's mistakes.

"Taylor, Sweetheart, Mama needs to talk to you. Let's go upstairs to your room."

My precious seven-year-old daughter followed me upstairs, where I sat down in a white rocker nestled in the corner of her room. As she flopped down on the floor near my feet, her big brown eyes looked up at me with wonder while she lightly bit the corner of her lip. This child was the first to teach me the meaning of unconditional love. I silently prayed, "Lord, please don't let me break her heart."

"This isn't easy for Mama, Taylor, but I need to tell you some things about myself. After my daddy died, I made lots of mistakes."

She sat ever so quietly as I told her that I had been married two other times before meeting her daddy. I paused to let her ask questions, but I was greeted only by silence. After what seemed like hours, she innocently cocked her little head to the side and said, "Does that mean you have three wedding dresses?"

"Well," I stammered through my shock, "yes, I did, but I gave the other two away."

She crawled up in my lap. Nothing else needed to be said.

Now I had to tell Austin. I decided to take him for a drive. Although he wasn't supposed to, I let him sit in the front seat with me as I drove around in our neighborhood. He looked so different than his sissy, with his blonde hair and blue eyes. When they were together, though, there was no mistaking they were siblings, especially when they laughed.

A memory flashed through my mind of when he decided to move away from home at age three. He had high-stepped into the kitchen, wearing a diaper and cowboy boots, holding tight to as many horses as he could carry. He announced, "I'm movin', Mama." I secretly hoped what I was about to tell him didn't cause him to think about moving again.

I started telling my second-born child that his mama had done some foolish things before meeting his daddy. Tears began to fall from my baby's eyes after telling him the truth.

Jesus, please help me, I thought to myself. "I'm so sorry, Austin. Please forgive Mama. I never intended to hurt you."

"But, Mama, that means I have two step-daddies."

"Is that why you are crying, son? No. No, you don't. You only have one daddy who loves you very much."

I had to pull over. I couldn't see to drive anymore.

When we returned, I tried to explain to Troy the weight that had been lifted from my shoulders. I felt like I wanted to dance, so that's what we did, all four of us in the kitchen. If this was a taste of freedom, I wanted more.

Nineteen

"Whenever you stand praying, forgive, if you have anything against anyone…"

Mark 11:25

I awoke early to the sunshine peeking through the windows and the sound of birds singing a melody. My heart skipped a beat after realizing this was the day that I would stand before the church and share my testimony. I slid from the bed quietly, so as not to wake Troy. I needed some alone time in the closet to pray.

Memorized note cards lay before me. I sat gazing at the words. I had given many presentations over the years at work; public speaking didn't scare me very much. However, I had never stood in front of thousands and admitted to living a masquerade.

"Lord, I'm scared. Yet I know this is what you are asking me to do. If someone comes closer to you because of my story, it will be worth it."

It seemed even the kids dressed quietly that morning. They knew it was a big day for their mama. We all hugged as we left the house.

Troy whispered, "I'm proud of you."

I made it down to the front row where I awaited Pastor Rick to give me my cue to walk up to the stage. Sitting behind me in the audience were friends of mine who were about to be handed a bombshell. I feared everyone would think I was dishonest when I confessed my life had been a web of deceit.

When I heard my name, I started toward the stairs, which felt like climbing Mt. Everest. I could hear my voice quiver as I began.

"I was asked to speak today because my life has recently been radically changed. Shame and guilt has caused me to pretend to be someone I wasn't for many years. There are some of you here today who have known me for a long time, yet you don't know the truth. You see…"

I looked out at people crying. Some bowed their heads with their own shame. Others stared into space, lost in thought. As I finished, a line of people formed thirty deep. I soon found out many of them were just like me, afraid of being judged.

All of these years, I thought I was alone in my pain, only to find out that the church is full of withering souls.

My friends questioned, "Why didn't you tell me? Nothing would have changed the love I have for you."

Their hugs told me that they meant what they said.

Leaving the church, hand in hand with my family, I pondered for a minute and thought about the Woman at the Well. Two thousand years separated our stories, yet we were very much alike—both divorced and ashamed. Yet after we met Jesus, we were never the same.

****

After arriving home, I decided to depart from my beloved closet and move to the basement. I needed more space. Jesus and I had work to do. I felt like an onion that had just been peeled and I knew it was only the first layer. I wanted to get to the core of who I was designed to be.

I sat in the corner with a single light by my side to illuminate my Bible. I wished I'd known the verses in the book of Psalms when I was growing up, which would have told me I was fearfully and wonderfully made, and how God put my tears in His bottle. It had to be a big bottle, for all my tears. *Lord, do you actually know the number of hairs on my head?* I questioned.

Psalm 139:16 says, "Your eyes have seen my unformed substance; And in Your book were all written the days that were ordained for me, when as yet there was not one of them."

Lord, this means you knew me even before I was born.

Jeremiah 29:11 says, "For I know the plans that I have for you, plans for welfare and not for calamity, to give you a future and a hope."

But, Lord, I had calamity.
Amos Ingle shot my daddy.
You could have prevented it.
My head was spinning. I had just stood before thousands and experienced a freedom that was hard to explain. I didn't want to think about Amos Ingle. I cried out, "I just want more of you, Lord."
Forgiveness.
"God, how am I supposed to forgive the man who killed my daddy? Furthermore, why did you allow it to happen? You could have prevented it. Why didn't you?" I questioned aloud.

I knew in my heart that I might not ever know the answer to that question this side of heaven, for He is God. Did I really think I knew what was best for me?

I turned off the light and laid in the dark, knowing it was time to deal with this matter. The bitterness of unforgiveness and all the times I questioned God was eating me alive, as though I was slowly drinking battery acid.

I closed my eyes and thoughts flooded my mind about all the good things that had happened since Daddy died. My mother married Howard Lee and they had been married for over twenty years. Mother had accepted the Lord as her Savior. Two of my uncles had been saved right after that dreadful day. Why had I not thought about those things before?

I remembered the story of Joseph from the book of Genesis. He had been left for dead by his brothers and then sold into slavery, later becoming an advisor to a king. Joseph learned that what was intended for evil, God used for good. Joseph trusted God.

I said aloud, "That's it, isn't it, Lord? You want me to trust you, even if I don't understand.

I could taste salt on my lips as the tears streamed.

I pulled my knees to my chest as I rolled on the floor. "Please, God! Oh please, God! Forgive me for questioning You."

I felt sick to my stomach as thoughts of Amos returned.

"Lord, did Amos Ingle ask You to forgive him of murder?"

Memories of when he sat beside me during the parole board meeting flashed through my mind. Amos had asked me if he could spend his dying days with his mother. He had been paroled shortly after by the governor and indeed been given the opportunity to be with his mother until he died.

That was a picture of a loving God.

I smiled at the thought. If Amos was indeed forgiven, he was in heaven with Jesus, leaving me here angry and wallowing in my own pain.

I laid on the carpet with my Bible clutched to my chest and I whispered, "I forgive you, Amos."

With those words, I could imagine chains falling from me, exposing another layer of freedom.

****

Later that week, I decided to drive to the cemetery where Amos was buried. I'm not sure why I felt the need, but I hoped it would increase the peace that was starting to invade my heart.

It was a beautiful day and memories of my daddy flooded my thoughts. I laughed aloud, thinking about how much I had loved going to square dances with him and Mother. There would be a couple hundred people dancing yet all eyes seemed to be upon the two of them as he swung her around. Joy came from the times I got to be his partner as he taught me to tap and slide my foot. Beads of sweat dripped from his forehead, but all I noticed was the smile that occupied his face.

Oh, I will never forget the night he took me out fox hunting with him. It was just the two of us, sitting by a roaring fire and listening for the dogs to catch the scent of a fox and start the chase. I couldn't believe he could name the dogs by their bark.

"That one is Loretta," he said.

"Daddy, why in the world did you name your dog Loretta?"

"Because she has a good mouth on her like Loretta Lynn."

His laughter echoed in the woods as he pulled out his pocketknife to whittle.

The sight of the white church on the Old Dover Road jerked me back to reality. The place Daddy took his last breath on this earth. I passed slowly, continuing to drive the curvy road that held so many memories, until I came upon the Ingle family cemetery.

Hesitantly, I opened the car door, unsure of all the emotions I was feeling. I walked around the tombstones, looking for the name that had caused such a tragic collision in my world.

Amos Ingle.

The gray stone sat before me. To my surprise, it was a double monument. Amos had been buried with his mother, who had died a short time after him. Inscribed on it were the words, *"Suffered on earth together, now we rest in heaven together."*

I felt the cool ground beneath my knees and the flow of tears from my eyes. Only God.

TWENTY

"Cease Thriving and Know that I am God."

Psalm 46:10

The definition of freedom is the state of not being imprisoned or enslaved. I had been in my own private bondage most of my life. The taste of freedom was sweet. To think that I had actually run from the One who had the keys to unlock the chains made no sense to me now. It's as though I had been given new eyes to see with God; I could experience the one thing I desired all along. I had both peace of mind and peace at heart. The bitterness and anger were gone.

Jesus Himself said, "Peace I leave with you; My peace I give to you; not as the world gives do I give to you. Do not let your heart be troubled, nor let it be fearful."

Forgiveness enabled me to receive what He offered.

****

Troy arrived home from a meeting at church just in time for dinner. I cherished the time around our table with the four of us. Conversations were always lively and this night was no exception.

"I'm going to the Ukraine on a missions trip," Troy announced happily.

"Wow! No fair!" cried our two adventurous children. "Can we come, too?"

I nipped that in the bud really quick. It was one thing for Troy to go halfway around the world, but to take my babies was a different story entirely.

"What are you going to be doing there, build?" I asked.

"Actually, no. There is a team of ten and we will be working in orphanages," Troy answered. He shared with us what he had learned at the meeting. "Communism fell in 1992, leaving people without jobs to provide for their families. The government provided food to the orphanages; therefore, desperate parents left their children in these institutions in order to provide food for their starving kids. At one time, there were more than 500,000 orphans in Ukraine alone. Rhonda, do you want to go this time? You love children."

"Nope. I will stay here and take care of our own."

Before long, his bags were packed once again. We were very proud of him and with anxious hearts awaited his return.

The two weeks passed quickly and it seemed Troy could not get his bags in the car fast enough. "I have so many things to share with you guys!" he exclaimed.

For a man of few words, he certainly spewed upon us that night. He described the joy and excitement of the children when the team arrived at each orphanage.

"We carried candy and stickers in our pockets and tried to communicate as best we could. Honestly, I think they just wanted to be held. Most were hungry for attention."

He described to Taylor and Austin how different their lives were from kids in America. Orphans shared clothes that were not washed. Their beds were all lined up in a row; no one had anything they could call their own. Food consisted mainly of potatoes and cabbage, and fruit was a special treat. He tried to explain the smells, but his emotions overcame him. The kids and I sat in silence.

Then he raised his head and announced, "I think we are supposed to adopt."

Taylor jumped up and down, screaming, "Yes! Remember my little friend in first grade from Russia? I have always wanted to adopt."

Austin chimed in, but I mentally shut down the chatter.

"Rhonda, what do you think?" Troy asked.

"Well, I think you are crazy. That's what I think. I'm forty-five years old and we have two beautiful, healthy children. Why would we want to adopt another child?"

"Will you pray about it?" Troy asked.

Ugh. What was I supposed to say to that? My mind slipped into a whirlwind. *Something could be wrong with an adopted child. Troy is going off the deep end. I'm not doing it.*

We laid in bed motionless. I couldn't think about anything except reasons why we should not adopt. Troy didn't push the subject, but how could I refuse to pray?

The next morning over coffee, Troy suggested that we visit our pastor, Rick, and his wife Patti. They had adopted an older child from the Ukraine when they were in their fifties. They also had two grown daughters, so their situation was similar to ours. I agreed to meet with them.

Rick was excited to talk with us. He said he rarely had the opportunity to discuss joyful subjects since most people visited him with problems. I knew about that all too well, but I wasn't convinced this was a joy-filled subject, either.

Our pastor had such a presence about him, so kind, warm, and full of wisdom. We had never before met privately with him, but after entering his office we enveloped ourselves in the softness of a large leather sofa that made it easy to bare our feelings.

He did not tell us we should or should not adopt. What he did tell us was to turn our request completely over to the Lord. He said to pray that the Lord would make apparent to us what we should do by opening doors wide or by slamming them shut in our faces. It made sense to me. I just wondered how God would be that obvious.

Together, we prayed simply and believed strongly.

Well, I'm here to say that God has a sense of humor. From the day we left Pastor Rick's office, conversations with others turned into discussions about adoption—and not from our own initiative. It didn't matter where we were or who we were with, the word *adopt* would just pop up out of nowhere.

One rainy, cold December day, Troy and I decided to do some Christmas shopping. We went to Target and he dropped me off at the front door while he parked. I stood in the glassed front entry, waiting for him to join me, when a man stopped to put on his jacket before going outside. I casually asked, "Are you doing some Christmas shopping today?"

To which he replied, "Yes, I am. For my two new adopted daughters."

I smiled and said nothing else. When Troy joined me he knew immediately that something was wrong from the expression on my face.

"You are not going to believe what happened," I said.

I shared my story and he just giggled, saying, "The Lord seems to be opening some doors pretty wide."

I knew God was trying to show me, but I was holding out for that moment when I knew He was trying to get my attention.

I had a dream that not only confirmed what we were to do, but it changed my life. I dreamt that Troy and I walked in the front door of our home holding a boy and girl in our arms and introduced them to Taylor and Austin for the first time. I awoke to the caress of tears, knowing the Lord had spoken.

I shook Troy, and through tears shared with him what had happened. God was indeed calling our family to adopt, and not just one child, but two—a young boy and girl.

The following morning, we sat Taylor and Austin down to talk with them about what it would mean to their lives if we actually adopted. Their eyes began to light up with excitement.

Austin said, "I want a brother."

Taylor said, "No. I want a sister."

Troy and I just looked at each other. Are we really going to adopt two?

This is a mistake. These kids have no idea how their lives will change. What are we doing? This is crazy.

Then I heard Troy say, "Well, you both are going to get what you want. We are going to adopt both a boy and girl."

Our children jumped up and down, screaming and clapping. I silently prayed that their joy would be contagious because I was shaking in my shoes.

There's no turning back now. Taylor and Austin would be so disappointed. What are we doing? How can I work with four kids? Troy can't go on any more missions trips. I mean it. He's done.

While Troy made a phone call to start the process, I went to the basement to pray.

****

Pastor Rick and Patti had used a nonprofit organization from Franklin to facilitate their adoption. We found out International House of Hope is not an actual adoption agency, but a nonprofit that purchases homes in the Ukraine for Christian families if the family agrees to adopt three or more orphans. It was a way to keep the children in their homeland. International House of Hope only assisted in a small number of adoptions per year since that was not their primary focus.

We trusted Pastor Rick and Patti, and they told us we would love Anna Walker and Andre Komar, who were the founders. Anna would be responsible for expediting our paperwork here in the states and Andre would take care of all our needs when we actually went to the Ukraine to adopt.

Our first step in the process was to meet Anna. I did not know what to expect in that meeting, and nothing could have prepared me for the wealth of information she needed to know about our lives. Sitting before us was a beautiful, soft-spoken blonde, not at all what I had envisioned. I thought surely the door would slam shut once she heard about my troubled past and multiple marriages. Surprisingly, International House of Hope agreed to facilitate our adoption.

The process was incredibly long and arduous, including FBI background checks, mountains of paperwork, and a lot of waiting. Once we received approval that we were fit parents and could provide a safe and financially secure home in the states, we could apply for adoption in the Ukraine. In our application, we applied to adopt a boy and a girl between the ages of four and seven.

The Ukrainian Adoption Center would have to grant us an appointment before plans could be made to enter the country. Days turned into months.

Waiting was so frustrating. Taylor and Austin didn't think it was going to happen. Every day they questioned when they would get their brother and sister.

Ukraine's procedure is quite different from other countries. We would actually get to choose which children we would bring into our family. Anna explained that when we received our appointment in the Kiev Adoption Center, books would be laid before us with pictures of children who were in orphanages.

There was one little stipulation. If a child had received any communication from a relative within 365 days, they could not be adopted. It didn't matter if it was a single phone call from a distant cousin of a cousin, the child could not be adopted.

Finding out the details of how the process worked caused anxiety. How in the world do you choose a child when there are so many to choose from? We knew it would be impossible to take Taylor and Austin with us, regardless of how hard it would be to leave them. Their list of attributes would be quite different from ours.

We took the time to meet with other parents who had adopted from Ukraine and asked, "How did you choose?"

Their answer was always the same. "God will tell you."

Faith and trust usually develop over time. It seemed God had placed us on a fast track to maturity. We were learning to lean on Him daily, and not our own understanding.

More time passed.

Our paperwork expired. We had to pay more money to update our documents. We questioned if God's hand was still in the midst of these barren days.

A year passed.

Everywhere we turned, people kept telling us that it was all in God's perfect timing. If there was one thing I learned through this experience, it was our timing and God's timing are not always one and the same.

And so we waited.

Twenty-One

"Ask, and it will be given to you; seek, and you will find; knock, and it will be opened to you."

Matthew 7:7

To wait causes distress. Waiting also opens the floodgate to doubts. I knew all too well.

God surely didn't mean for us to adopt.

I knew I needed to stop these thoughts. *Why do I question God?* The battle in my head continued and I couldn't stop it, no matter how hard I tried.

The kids left for school and Troy had an early morning meeting, leaving me alone at my desk to catch up on paperwork. However, the assault on my mind rendered me incapable. I stared blankly at the computer screen in front me as random pictures from our files changed every fifteen seconds.

The toothless smiles and silly grins on Taylor and Austin's faces usually made me smile. Not today. I bowed my head to pray. I was weary from waiting and I was sick to death of all the people asking when the children were going to come. "I don't know!" I screamed aloud, as though someone could hear me. I could feel my breathing grow deeper and the warmth of tears on my cheeks.

I opened my eyes and before me was a picture that Troy had taken of three orphans while in Ukraine. I was looking into the eyes of two little girls and a boy who would melt anyone's heart; then the picture faded into another.

"No. Please, no. I want to see their faces!" I cried out.

I searched frantically for the same picture, but to no avail. I slid from my chair to my knees.

"Lord, why is this taking so long? Please, Lord, I'm begging you. We are all so tired. Why did You bring us this far only to make us wait? We trusted you."

One hour passed.

I heard the ping of an incoming email. I arose and with one single click I read these words:

Dear Mr. and Mrs. Troy Madge:

You have an appointment at the Ukrainian Adoption Center. Plan to depart for the Ukraine on Easter Sunday, April 11, 2004. I will be in touch shortly with additional information.

Regards,
Andre Komar

****

After eighteen months of waiting, the door had opened. We had less than two weeks to prepare for our departure to the Ukraine. Although we'd had months to plan for this very day, there were a lot of last-minute details.

The week prior to our farewell happened to be Taylor and Austin's spring break. We decided to squeeze in a small family vacation to the Smokey Mountains, knowing it was the last time together we'd have as a family of four.

Life will never be the same.

I had to choose to take those thoughts captive. *We are going to be a family of six with much to look forward to*, I said to myself over and over.

But it wasn't only me allowing reality to settle in. Taylor and Austin were overwhelming us with questions. It was understandable. We had never been apart from them longer than a week and we were told to plan to be gone for thirty days. That's a long time to be separated from your parents. Not to mention, when we returned they would have to share us with two new siblings.

I'm not sure if I could have left them had it not been for Mother, my pillar of strength. She agreed to live in our home and care for the children while we were away, regardless of how long it took.

****

Easter Sunday arrived. Our flight didn't depart until 1:05 in the afternoon, allowing us time for sweet family traditions. It was obvious we were all trying to be strong for one another as we eyed the hands of the clock.

We were filled with excitement, sadness, joy, fear, happiness, thankfulness—a windstorm of emotions. Yet how does one express their mental state with such a range of feelings?

No words were necessary, really. We sat in the middle of the floor and held on to one another as though our lives depended upon it.

The time came to say good-bye as we gathered in the entryway to hold hands and pray. I knew in my heart our circle was bonded by the love of our Heavenly Father.

Troy prayed, "Lord, please shield us and bring us back safely to our children. We trust You will lead us to the ones You have chosen."

I looked Taylor and Austin in the eyes, and as I told them how much I loved them, my heart ached sorely with every word. We all embraced as long as possible, knowing that our friends, who had asked if they could take us to the airport, were waiting in the driveway.

As we walked to the car, we turned back to see Taylor's face pressed against the window. Troy blew her a kiss and her little hand returned the gesture. Austin, face red from crying, stood in the doorway, waving frantically. Mother had her arms around them to keep them from running after us.

After loading our two fifty-pound bags into the trunk of the car, we crawled in the backseat. We turned one last time to look at our babies as the car slowly backed out of our driveway. It seemed more than my heart could bear. I laid my head on Troy's shoulder, unable to contain myself any longer. Sounds of weeping filled the car.

What are we doing?

****

The hum of the plane overtook the thoughts running through my mind. I looked out the window and tightly gripped Troy's hand. It was hard to believe that every moment we flew farther away from the familiar, we moved closer to the unknown. Neither of us spoke very much, nor did we sleep.

Not in a million years would I have ever believed we would be flying to Ukraine to adopt two children. We were two broken people with less than stellar pasts, but God had chosen us for this purpose. Trust. I was learning to trust.

Our itinerary took us from Nashville to Washington D.C., to Vienna, and finally to Kiev, Ukraine. As we set foot on foreign ground, my heart beat faster. The Bible says to pray continually. For the first time in my life, I understood why.

Andre was supposed to pick us up. It was strange to be so dependent upon someone we'd never met. We were told he was a rather large, strong-looking man with sandy-colored hair.

We made our way to the baggage claim area, but Andre was not to be found. I sensed that everyone was looking at us oddly. I laughed and said to Troy, "Toto, we aren't in Kansas anymore."

He didn't find my humor very funny, but it was because of him that we were getting so much attention.

Troy likes new white tennis shoes, and he was sporting a brand-new pair just for the trip. The problem was that Ukrainians did not wear anything other than dark footwear. You could see them snicker as they looked at his feet.

"Rhonda and Troy, over here," a voice yelled. The guy did not fit the description of Andre, but it was certainly nice to hear our names.

"I'm Andre," he introduced himself.

Troy was skeptical and alarmed because we were carrying a lot of cash. I could tell from his face that he was concerned.

Obviously, Andre saw the fear, as well, and said, "I'm not Andre Komar. My name just happens to also be Andre. Why don't you call me Little Andre?"

As we waited on our luggage, Troy leaned over and whispered in my ear, "I'm not sure I trust this guy. What if this is all a scam to take our cash?"

"Troy, we are going to have to trust God in this," I whispered as I took his hand in mine and squeezed it tightly, trying to calm myself as much as him.

We made our way outside and found the car. We got in the backseat as Little Andre began to tell us his testimony. "I was once a pickpocket."

Troy jerked his head toward me and whispered, "See? I knew we shouldn't trust this guy."

I hit his leg and reached into my bag to find a piece of paper. I scribbled a note: *"Troy, he wouldn't tell us if he was going to take our money."*

I wasn't born yesterday.

Little Andre took us to a very small yet clean apartment. Every square inch served a purpose, from the compact kitchen to the living room with a pull-out sofa for our bed. He left us to rest and said that "Big Andre" would pick us up for breakfast the next morning.

We collapsed on the makeshift bed, but not before we prayed. We knew we had to completely depend upon God. There was no other way.

We had heard so much about Andre Komar and couldn't wait to meet him. He arrived right on time, and the second he walked through the door, Troy and I both exhaled our anxieties. We knew immediately we could trust him.

We drove to a local restaurant called Arizona Barbeque. I guess Andre was trying to make us feel more at home. I ordered bacon and eggs and Troy decided upon sausage and eggs, both of us thinking we should keep it simple.

My stomach churned a bit when the waitress sat an iron skillet before me with barely cooked, thick pieces of fat covered two jiggly eggs. Troy's plate was straight from a *Tom and Jerry* cartoon, with two eggs in the center surrounded by hotdogs linked together.

It wasn't in our nature to complain, so we picked at our food with gag reflexes on high alert. Coffee brought relief as Andre shared that he was once a high-ranking government official under communist rule in Ukraine. I could just envision him in his uniform.

"Andre, how in the world did you meet Anna?" I asked.

He explained when their country gained their independence from Russia, he was put in charge of planning a day of celebration for their country, much like our Fourth of July. "I'm sure you have heard Anna has a Ukrainian heritage and is fluent in our language, plus she is a wonderful singer. I felt she was the perfect person to perform at our celebration. It didn't matter to me that she traveled with Billy Graham, performing at his conferences. Her music provided love, and I knew that's what my people needed." He continued, "Interestingly enough, I didn't understand God's plan when I invited Anna back the following year."

Andre explained that in the course of their friendship, he accepted Jesus into his heart and stepped down from the government. The two of them, along with Anna's husband James, formed International House of Hope.

I could tell that Troy had relaxed after hearing Andre's story. How could you not have confidence in someone with a testimony like his?

Andre told us to take the afternoon to buy a few groceries for the apartment and catch up on some rest. He said, "Tomorrow is a big day. One that you have waited for a long time."

We walked the cobblestone streets that afternoon, mesmerized by the sights and sounds. When we flew in, it appeared that Kiev was a large, inviting city. Up close, we could see the ravages of communism. Buildings were without repair and weeds grew upon the sidewalks. Tall buildings served as apartments that had housed families for decades.

Growing up in the South, we were raised to be hospitable to those we met, always giving a warm smile and firm handshake. Our Southern charm did not seem to be very effective in Kiev. Most people walked with their heads bowed, and regardless of how hard we tried, they would not respond to our charisma.

These people had lost hope long ago, and therefore joy. The country was only in the beginning stages of recouping from the fall of Communism. The middle class did not exist, only extreme wealth or poverty. The average salary was a hundred and fifty dollars per month, and vodka could be bought for the same price as a bottle of water, contributing to high rates of alcoholism. The looks on their faces were filled with despair for what tomorrow could bring.

We found a grocery store and felt like children trying to figure out what to purchase based on pictures from the food containers. It was much safer to purchase fresh items, so our first night we made chicken breast sautéed in olive oil, with fresh bread and cheese.

After dinner, we snuggled in bed, gripped hands, and prayed.

"Please, Lord, let us hear from you. Make it clear which children You have chosen for our family."

Amen.

TWENTY-TWO

"Trust in the Lord with all your heart and do not lean on your own understanding."

Proverbs 3:5

My eyes opened to the warmth of sunshine on my face. Today was the day we'd been waiting years for.

"Troy, wake up."

As the anticipation of our appointment grew keener, my heart began to beat faster. Troy and I sat in silence, forcing down scrambled eggs and slightly burned toast lathered in butter. Butter makes everything better.

A gentle knock at the door interrupted the quiet. Andre greeted us with bear hugs. How did he know that's what I desperately needed? "Let's go," he said.

Our ride to the adoption center was short, and we soon found ourselves in front of a large stone building. A wooden stairway led us to a small room lined with chairs. Andre walked up to a small window in the wall and began a conversation in their own language.

Troy and I took a seat among other couples. I didn't expect to see so many people in the same place for the same purpose. All the women were checking out what each other were wearing. Typical women, feeling competitive.

What if they get called back first? Could they choose the child I want?

Trust.

"Andre Komar?"

He arose and motioned for us to join him. A dark-haired, middle-aged woman greeted us and waved toward the three seats positioned in front of her desk. Before us were binders filled with pictures of children, all needing a mother and father.

After Andre explained that the director did not speak English, the two of them began a long, intense conversation. They were determining the future of our family and we had no idea what they were saying.

Finally, she stood and stepped out of the room.

"They do not have a boy and girl sibling pair that are ready for international adoption," Andre explained.

"How can that be? Look at all these pictures," Troy replied.

I felt sick.

Andre said with a smile, "Don't worry. Be happy."

It was not the time for jokes. I could tell Troy was uptight; his clenched jaw gave him away.

The director reentered the room with two pictures in her hands; both were of girls.

Andre told us, "These are two very healthy sisters, ages three and four. The director is allowing us to visit these girls as a gift to me because we have known each other for many years."

"But, Andre, we have promised Austin a brother. We do not want two girls. What about all the children in these books? Surely there is a brother and sister who need adopting?" I implored as calmly as possible.

"It would be very impolite and disrespectful if we do not see these girls. The children in these books do not fit the criteria in your application."

In other words, we had no choice.

Is God closing a door? What if we have come all this way for nothing? How would we ever explain this to Taylor and Austin? I know in my dream there was a boy and a girl.

After a quick bite to eat we headed to a village called White Church. Outside of Kiev the poverty was very apparent. As we drove slowly into town, we crossed over a bridge lined with people selling large cloth bags, filled tightly and tied closed.

"Andre, what are they selling?" I asked.

"There is a sugar beet factory here. These employees actually get paid with sugar. They are then required to sell the sugar in order to make money. The bags are filled with sugar."

An older woman swept the sidewalk with a broom made from sticks as another knelt on her knees to cut weeds with a sickle. I felt as though we had stepped back fifty years in time.

Wrought-iron gates slowly opened after we identified ourselves and the director met us at the door leading to his office. He was skeptical of us after reading our application.

"Why would you want to adopt two more children when you already have two?" he questioned.

Andre translated Troy's words. "We are a family of faith and we feel God has asked us to adopt."

He arose from his chair and walked out of the room, leaving us uncertain of whether or not our answer had satisfied his concern. We sat in silence as the smell of cabbage and bleach filled the room.

The turn of the door handle brought us to attention, and in a unified motion we watched two little girls enter the room. They were dressed in matching sailor dresses with large, white bows sitting atop their short, blonde hair.

Troy and I knelt down before them to get at their level. We smiled into little round faces with eyes as blue as the sky.

Andre translated, "This is Johnna, age four, and her sister, Valerie, age three. Johnna loves to pretend she is an actress and Valerie sings."

We brought them each a small stuffed animal, and as we placed one in each of their hands, they reached in their pockets to give us a piece of candy. An odd feeling came over the room as the director told Andre it was time for lunch and began to usher the girls out.

Johnna began to cry. I picked her up and stroked her hair. As I held her, it dawned on me that I felt no emotion. Actually I felt numb. I looked at Troy as he looked at me.

The director led the girls out of the room.

Andre said, "Let's go have coffee."

Troy and I walked ahead arm in arm to have a minute alone. "What just happened, Troy? I'm a mother. I should have felt something when that child started to cry. My heart was as dry as my eyes."

"Rhonda, we have to remember what Pastor Rick and others told us. They said God would reveal which children we are to have. Based on that, we have to assume Johnna and Valerie are not to be our daughters."

"How do we say no to two babies who need a mother and father? They have already faced so much rejection."

Andre joined us, aware of our apprehension. Troy tried to explain how we felt frozen from emotion.

Andre argued, "You don't seem to understand that these are two healthy, beautiful girls. Let's eat something and give you time to think. You will change your mind."

I knew Troy needed to handle this. He stated rather firmly, "Andre, lunch is not going to change our minds. You yourself told us we would know which children we were to adopt. We felt nothing in that room. We had stone-cold hearts—not just me, but Rhonda, also."

Andre looked at me as I nodded in agreement and said, "This isn't easy to say no. But we are following our hearts, Andre. Please try to understand."

We drove back to Kiev in silence as Andre made phone calls explaining that we needed another appointment. Thankfully, they agreed to see us again on Monday morning. As we got out of the car, Andre suggested we rest over the weekend and spend time in prayer.

The second we stepped into the apartment we collapsed into puddles of tears. I had never experienced anything so strange in my entire life; to be in a situation, strangled from sensation, when normally I'm gushing buckets of tears for the children around me.

What if we have made a mistake? What if Andre was right? I'm so confused. What have we done?

My damp pillow welcomed sleep as I repeated over and over again, "Lord, please help us."

I awakened to the sounds of Troy's deep breathing—a welcomed sound, knowing he carried the additional burden of being the leader of our family, and I was afraid he would be unable to sleep.

I reached for my Bible, hoping to find comfort from the confusion and doubts. My fingers found Ephesians 1:11, "...having been predestined according to His purpose who works all things after the counsel of His will."

I read it again, pausing on the words *predestined, purpose,* and *His will.* I honestly could not believe what I was reading. *Why do I question you, Lord? And why is it so hard to trust you?*

Troy stirred from his slumber, and before I could share what I had just read, he said, "Let's go visit the American couple who lives here, Jon and Luanne Mohr. Remember me telling you about them? I think it's just what we need."

He called them and they were happy to have us join them for the weekend.

Jon, Luanne, and their six children had lived in the Ukraine for some time as missionaries. An hour-long train ride would take us to their small village, Vinnitsa, which was much like White Church.

I forced my thoughts away from the little blonde angels who had stood before us. *I can't believe we turned away those babies. I feel heartless. We could have changed the course of their lives and we said no.*

Stop it! I wanted to scream. I had to stop thinking about them.

The heaviness sunk in. I missed Taylor and Austin terribly, and to make matters worse, it was expensive to call home and Internet usage was limited, making communication difficult. All of my questions led to more fear.

I knew Troy was lost in his own thoughts. The gentle touch of his hand brought some comfort.

We pulled into the station and were greeted by a family as happy to see us as we were to see all of them. It had been some time since they'd been with other Americans. The conversation was robust, but I fell back into my old state of pretending that the smile on my face was real. My heart cracked and tears flowed from the inside, yet no one knew.

Gathering around their table made me miss home, but when Luanne sat steak fajitas made with homemade tortillas in front of us, I began to feel much better. The food was plentiful and the laughter rang throughout the house. Troy was right; this is just what we needed.

After their children went to bed, we were able to share with Jon and Luanne about the prior day's events. As missionaries who were accustomed to listening to the heartache of others, they exuded wisdom in their words and warmth in their embrace.

The double-sized bed and squeaky mattress enveloped our tired bodies. We were asleep within minutes, but the smell of bacon and fresh coffee jolted us awake early the next morning. The Mohrs had planned a day to escape from the worries of the world. First stop—Hitler's bunker.

Their large, commercial-sized van took us easily on our adventure. Troy and I both expected a public park made famous by Hitler himself. Instead, we drove down a gravel road through a forest that led to a clearing. Jon knew the area well and walked us to an old Olympic-sized swimming pool nestled among the trees. He explained the pool was built specifically for Hitler to exercise when his army was in hiding.

Astonished, we walked a bit farther until Jon pointed down toward a grassed area. Unsure of what we were to see, we stepped closer. We saw a metal ladder eerily leading somewhere underground. My wildest imagination could not fathom what was beneath the soil on which we stood.

Hitler had built this private, secure area for him and his cohorts during the war. The bunker had been bombed and the remnants left only vague reminders of what once was.

With the history lesson over, the Mohrs decided it was time for a game of softball. What would Hitler have thought about the invasion upon his private world? For a while that day, we turned his forsaken field into a place of laughter and joy.

After dinner, Jon decided we would worship the next morning in their home. "I really feel as though we need to pray with you instead of going to a Ukrainian church only to be lost in the language."

The Spirit of God decided to join us that Sunday morning. The Mohrs' daughter played the piano as we sang familiar hymns. After scripture was read, Jon prayed for our clarity and clear direction in the coming days. Suddenly he said, "Do either of you know someone named Ruth?"

I froze. "That's my mother," I said.

"It's okay. Don't fear, Rhonda. Just pray for her continued good health and patience with the children."

What if something happens to my mother and we are twenty hours away? She's not used to living anywhere other than the farm. I've already lost my daddy. I can't lose her, too.

Jon could obviously see the concern through my tears. "Rhonda, the Lord says to lean upon Him and not your own understanding."

I knew I was supposed to, but I was still in the infant stages of trust.

I whispered, "Lord, I'm scared. I'm so scared…"

Twenty-Three

"I will not leave you as orphans; I will come to you."

John 14:18

With renewed vigor, we arrived back in Kiev to prepare for our second appointment at the adoption center. Andre left a message that he would pick us up the following morning promptly at eight o'clock.

We awoke early to pray. Actually, to beg God to help us. Soon after we walked outside to the curb, Andre drove up.

"Good morning! Today is the day the Lord hath made. Today is April the nineteenth." Andre announced.

I gasped. "Troy, Daddy died on April 19. We are going to see our children today. I just know it." *Could God have orchestrated this to bring joy on such a dark day in my life?* I wondered. *Is this what everyone means by His perfect timing?*

We pulled into the parking lot with expectant hearts. Eagerly, we walked up the steps of the adoption center in anticipation of what the Lord had planned. We took our seats as Andre spoke privately to the adoption center director.

He walked back and said, "Let's go. We need to come back tomorrow." *What? No.* "Andre, why?" I asked.

"The director cannot meet with us today and she asked that we come back at the same time tomorrow. Don't worry. Be happy. It will be fine."

The Lord didn't have a plan for this day after all. It's another day lost away from Taylor and Austin. I am tired of this game.

Knowing we were upset, Andre drove us to an Internet café so we could write an email home. Explaining that our appointment got pushed back one more day wasn't the news I wanted to deliver. Two weeks was beginning to feel like two years.

After Andre took us back to our home away from home, we got our Bibles and headed to a park. It was a beautiful afternoon, even with a slight chill. We were lost in our own thoughts and sought solace on a park bench.

The buds on the trees were beginning to bloom, making my heart long to see the dogwoods and redbuds blooming in Tennessee. The dogwoods were in full bloom when Daddy died—strange to mix such beauty with death.

> I read Isaiah 61:3: "'To grant those who mourn in Zion, Giving them a garland instead of ashes, The oil of gladness instead of mourning, The mantle of praise instead of a spirit of fainting.'"

The cool breeze blew across my face as I repeated that verse over and over in my mind. I wanted to scream.

Why did You get our hopes up? I just knew something good would happen on this terrible day. Where is our praise instead of despair? I don't understand, Lord.

I took a deep breath and turned to John 14:14. "'If you ask Me anything in My name, I will do it.'"

Lord, in your powerful name, I pray we see our children tomorrow.

****

The birds woke us early to prepare once more for another appointment. I was scared of being disappointed again. There was only one thing left to do—trust. Climbing the stairs for the third time, my clunky heels announced our arrival. We thought it was odd to find the waiting room empty, but we were greeted immediately.

Excitement stirred in the air as the director spoke to Andre in their native tongue. It sounded like they were giggling.

"Rhonda and Troy, yesterday the paperwork arrived in this office for a brother and sister from the Donetsk region. We could not bring you in for the appointment because the documents needed to be prepared."

Yesterday, April 19. My heart quivered. *Lord, I'm sorry I questioned You.*

The director laid two tiny pictures before us. Andre said, "This is Roman, age five, and his sister, Victoria, age six. Would you like to see them?"

Troy and I nodded through our tears. I picked up the pictures and glanced into the faces of two children, both void of expression. Victoria's hair looked much like my childhood Barbie dolls after I'd given them a haircut. Roman had deep, dark circles under his eyes that betrayed a profound sadness. Yet strangely, their beauty was captivating.

As we walked out of the center, Troy stopped to read a plaque hanging on the wall, which had 1 Samuel 1:27 written on it: "'For this boy I prayed, and the Lord has given me my petition which I asked of Him.'"

God's faithfulness was overwhelming. I realized that once again I had questioned the Lord. *I'm so sorry, Lord. Teach me to trust without questioning, please.*

Andre shifted into high gear by arranging a visit to meet the children in a village called Slavyansk within the Donetsk Region, nearly eight hundred miles away. We were told to pack a small bag of clothes for a few days' visit. The majority of our travel would be via train, but not just any ordinary train. The jewel we were to travel on for eighteen hours was from World War II.

To say we felt we were on an adventure would be an understatement, especially when Andre walked us to our cabin. We passed a man sitting alone at a small table with four chairs, smoking a cigarette while nursing a bottle of vodka. He turned our way with a drunken smile to welcome us on the journey.

Andre looked at us and said he would return shortly. Smoke rings filled the room as the man puffed and slurred some unknown words. I looked at Troy and said, "This may very well be the longest eighteen hours of our life."

The cramped cabin was meant for four, preferably small, people. Andre joined our party and enlightened us about this man who desperately needed a shower and toothbrush. Again Andre said, "Don't worry, be happy," as he winked and conversed with the stranger.

Troy asked, "What does he do for a living?"

"Oh, he's a pilot. He is headed home to visit family."

We laughed, thankful to be on a train. Suddenly, the conductor appeared and told Andre to follow him. Unbeknownst to us, Andre had been working behind the scenes to change our accommodations. He led us to a new cabin with four bunk beds. Sitting on the bottom of one of the bunks was a younger man and older woman.

Andre told us, "I will not be able to stay in a room with you because the train is overcrowded. This is a mother and her son, who are traveling together for her protection. They are from Israel and do not speak any English. Please don't worry about anything. It is almost time for bed and you all will sleep."

Troy and I sat next to each other on the bottom bunk, facing these two strangers, unable to say a word. We gazed out the window to ease the awkwardness. Acres upon acres of unused farmland raced past us, making us wonder why large combines and tractors sat in these fields, rusting away. Troy noticed there were no fences anywhere to be seen.

We took a little walk to find Andre and ask about these oddities. He was only a couple of cabins down from us; we had learned to trust that he was never far away.

"Well," he said, "the majority of farmland is owned by the government, so there isn't any need for fences. They own the equipment, as well. When communism fell, all farming came to a halt. The big pieces of machinery you see are actually sitting where they were last used, rusting away. People do not have money to purchase the land because there are no jobs."

So fascinating and yet so terribly sad I thought to myself as something stirred deeply inside me. I suddenly understood why Troy wanted to travel on his missions trips. Reading about other countries is quite different from actually being there. *I can't go on missions trips, though. I need to work when we get home. Troy is gifted with skills to build. There isn't anything I could do.*

We made it back to our cabin quickly and nestled back on our bunk. The old metal train had become rather chilly. Our dark-haired roommate smiled as she watched us. I could only imagine what she must be thinking. Her handsome son seemed less intrigued.

A short time later, as night approached, the son stood and used his coat as a drape to give his mother privacy while she changed into pretty pink pajamas. Maneuvering around, they lowered the top bunk; they made their beds just as though they were home. With tenderness, he helped his mother climb under the covers before hopping up on his top bunk. It wasn't long before the click-itty-clack of the train caught rhythm with his snores.

Troy stood to pull our top bunk down and see what bedding was available. Bundled together were small pillows stained from years of usage, folded pillowcases, and some sheets and wool blankets, much like the ones I had seen in army surplus stores.

"Let's make our beds, Rhonda."

I can't do it. I cannot lie beneath that wool blanket and put my head on that pillow. We could catch lice or scabies. No way.

I voiced my concern and Troy said, "Fine, but you are going to freeze to death while I sleep. I'll see you in the morning."

Troy wrestled with the cover and hopped up on his bunk while I lied down, pulling my knees to my chest in a fetal position. I opened my eyes and noticed that the sweet woman lying across from me, all snuggled and warm, was staring right at me.

She thinks I'm an idiot. Worse. She thinks that I won't lie under these blankets because I'm too good to do so. *Well, isn't that the case?*

I closed my eyes and prayed, "Lord, I'm so confused. Am I supposed to trust You enough to protect me from disease if I pull that blanket up over me?"

Sleep overtook me while I waited for an answer.

Soon the sun peeked through the window and the movement of the train caused me to stir. I awoke to find our cabin mates dressing.

Troy chuckled and said, "Are you warm down there? I'm nice and toasty up here."

I almost said something that I would have regretted when a knock on the door stopped me. Andre had brought hot tea.

"Bless you, Andre!" I squealed.

While sipping my tea, my unnamed bunkmate pulled a plum from her purse and held it out toward me. Cradled in the palm of her hand, this plump piece of fruit was a gift offering. I remembered the small bottles of lotions in my purse I had brought for the orphanage employees. Reciprocating, I opened the lotion and put a small amount in my own hand first to show her what it was. The smell of gardenia filled our cabin as our soft hands embraced one another. It was strange to think I would never see her again.

As the train slowed, my heart quickened. We were about to meet our children. Troy took my hand in his as we followed Andre off the train. I needed the stability; my knees were shaking.

Twenty-Four

"But now faith, hope, love, abide these three; but the greatest of these is love."

1 Corinthians 13:13

S lavyansk was a small town bordering Russia, where the evidence of war lingered. Windows were boarded and weeds grew where flowers once bloomed. Darkness hung in the air. Houses, old and weathered, used their yards as gardens to provide food. A wagon pulled by a team of oxen and an old cow tied to the back stopped to let us pass by. It seemed the eighteen-hour train ride had transported us back in time yet again.

Slowly we pulled down a dirt road that lead us to gates overgrown with bushes. Could this be where the children live?

Andre hopped out of the car and entered through a small entrance on the side of the building. He returned with an older, well-dressed woman.

"I would like you to meet the director of the orphanage, Mama Luba," Andre announced.

Troy and I extended our hands to greet this lovely woman. When our hands touched, we looked deeply into one another's eyes. Her warm, genuine smile brought reassurance. She asked Andre to share with us that she had done the best she could for the children with what the government had provided.

We walked toward the building. The anticipation felt much like entering the delivery room to await a child's birth, except that these two children we waited for were birthed from our hearts.

The scent of cabbage wafted through the air as we walked down the hallway. Mama Luba and Andre conversed. Unsure of what they were saying, Troy and I assumed their laughter was an indication she liked us.

I found myself curious about this woman as we took our seats in her office. Andre shared with us that she had been a director for over twenty years. She appeared to be in her fifties, with blonde hair, stylishly bobbed. Her suit was extremely well fitted and matched her pumps and stockings. I wondered how she could afford such a nice outfit.

There was a knock at the door.

Victoria and Roman entered the room. Their beauty was magnetic. I slowly dropped to my knees, taking in every bit of this sacred moment; I heard Troy catch his breath as he bent down beside me. The tears began to flow.

Victoria stood before us proudly; on her head was the largest bow I had ever seen. It was about the size of a pie. Mama Luba had dressed her in the finest she had to offer—a short gold dress with trim that looked as if it had once been white.

Roman bowed his head shyly, but the corners of his lip curled upward, revealing a slight smile. He had outgrown his pants, but he rubbed the front of his shirt as though to say he was extremely proud.

It was hard not to touch them. We inched forward toward them.

Andre asked the children, "Why do you think these people are here?"

Victoria replied, "To make our picture."

"No, Victoria. This couple would like to be your mama and your papa. Would you both like to go to America with them?"

"*Da!*" they screamed delightedly.

There was not one single second of hesitation. These children had no idea who we were or where they were going. It didn't matter to them; they were getting a mama and papa.

Through tears and smiles, Troy gave Roman a teddy bear with a red-checkered bow and I handed Victoria a doll with blonde curls and a turquoise dress. Mama Luba told Andre it was probably the first time they had ever received a gift all their own.

As their eyes widened with wonder, Andre explained, "Victoria and Roman, you are not only going to have a mama and papa, but a brother and sister. You will live in a house with your own room and you will have a dog named Star. You are also going to get a new name. Victoria, you will now be Rachel. Roman, you will now be called Luke."

To this announcement Roman replied, "I want to be Rachel."

We burst into laughter.

Luke jumped into my arms and Rachel hugged Troy. Our hearts erupted.

Troy reached into his bag to get candy and handed them each one apiece. Luke quickly put his in his pocket, so Troy gave him another piece. He put it in the other pocket. Troy opened a piece and popped it in his mouth. Luke loved this game, but Victoria wanted her turn. Afterward, they took our hands and lead us to where they slept.

Knowing we couldn't understand them, they exaggerated their actions and talked slowly, thinking that would help communication. We entered a room with twenty beds lined in back-to-back rows. Luke showed us how he had made his bed without a wrinkle.

Andre joined us and announced it was time to leave. He told us to take some photos with our Polaroid camera so we could place the pictures under the children's pillows while we were away. It seemed we had just met and were already having to promise to return in the morning. It wasn't easy to leave.

We went to dinner with Andre and celebrated the day's events while he explained what he had learned about the children.

"It appears their mother lost her parental rights a little over three years ago. Neighbors found them abandoned in an apartment with no food or water; neither were wearing adequate clothing. It is believed they were alone for four to five days. Medical records indicate they are healthy and I'm sure you noticed there are no visible signs of fetal alcohol syndrome, which is wonderful."

I asked, "What is known about the mother? Was she married? Do they have the same father?"

"The mother was nineteen when she had Victoria and gave birth to Roman 358 days later. The same father is listed on the birth certificates, but the chances of that are pretty slim."

"They seem healthy, except for their teeth. They are bad. Do you think they even know what a dentist is?" Troy asked.

"It's hard to say. The problem is most children in orphanages don't get milk to drink, only juice and tea."

I couldn't help but ask about Mama Luba. "How could she afford such a nice suit, Andre?"

"She probably saved over a year for that one outfit. I expect that you will see her wear it again. Let's shift gears and talk about what you should expect the next few days."

Andre explained that we would spend the following morning with the children and then prepare to travel back to Kiev so he could start working through the massive amount of paperwork. He had already arranged for a court date with the judge in Slavyansk. In one week our adoption would be the first international adoption to occur within the village.

We got back to our hotel and tried to wrap our heads around the fact that we had just seen our two new children. It was shocking to me that they were not the least bit afraid.

"Troy, I cannot come close to believing how God brought all this together. We applied for a boy and girl between the ages of four and seven. They became adoptable on the anniversary of the day Daddy died. When you align with God's plans, anything can happen."

Troy replied, "Well, the Bible says, 'All things are possible with God.' Witnessing firsthand makes it easier to believe."

We laid together in our small hotel room, reminiscing about our young son and daughter until sleep took over.

The second the alarm sounded, we jumped from bed. Andre knocked on our door an hour later, all smiles. After strong coffee and toast, we headed back to where Luke Roman and Rachel Victoria awaited.

Mama Luba embraced us at the door. Andre was right; she was wearing the same outfit. Bless her heart. However, my concentration shifted elsewhere as the sound of giggles and little running feet caused us to turn toward the stampede headed our way.

I picked up Luke as he gargled words at me. "Andre, please tell me what he said!"

"I love you already!"

Why did I worry with makeup? Troy took Rachel by the hand as we wandered our way through a mass of orphans, all speaking gibberish to our listening ears. One redheaded darling grabbed Troy's leg. Rachel became defensive, her eyes of anger pushing the child away.

"Andre, what happened? What did the child say to upset Rachel?"

"He asked if you could be his daddy, too. Rachel said, 'No! He is my daddy.'"

My heart.

We made our way to a playroom filled with toys. Luke and Rachel were overjoyed to see this shrine of gifts to be used only for special occasions, such as today. It was sad to think about the other sixty orphans who could be playing with these hidden treasures.

Andre and Mama Luba left us alone to play so they could get started on paperwork. Not knowing how to converse, we amused them with silliness. It suddenly hit me: Rachel was not coming near me; she chose Troy.

"Honey, Rachel seems to keep her distance from me."

"Give her time. Maybe she associates you with her biological mother who left her. I imagine it will be hard to trust."

The lure of pink fingernail polish made perfect bait. After pulling it from my purse and polishing my own nails, she sat next to me, pulling off shoes and socks to reveal ten little unwashed toes. I suppose she thought I needed a closer look because she leaned back to position her foot right in my face.

Memories flooded my mind of holding Taylor and Austin's feet for the first time, counting toes and kissing their soles till they squirmed. Now, before me, my daughter offered her feet. Gently, I cradled each foot in my hand for the first time and painted color over soil. She seemed awed when I blew deep breaths of air on each nail to quicken the drying process. I looked deeply into her eyes, but the darkness revealed nothing. I smiled. She ran.

But what if she never trusts me? What would I do if this child chose to keep me at arm's length? How easy would it be to love if not loved in return?

Trust would need to be established before love would come. I knew that all too well. Before I loved God, I learned to trust Him first.

Andre joined us to translate as we shared pictures from our life. The fascination on their faces was priceless when they saw Taylor and Austin's pictures for the first time. They wanted to know how old they were and if they went to school.

Andre explained, "Yes, they go to school and you both will, also. Kids in America have to in order to learn to read and write."

They had no idea what awaited them.

Andre began to fidget, indicating he had a lot on his mind. Suddenly, he clapped his hands together and said, "Okay, let's talk. As we discussed earlier, it is customary to purchase the orphanage a gift. Do you have any thoughts about what you might like to buy?"

The makeshift playground outside was completely unsafe. We asked Andre what the cost of new equipment would be.

He suggested that we talk to Mama Luba and get her opinion. After she joined us and Andre told her what we wanted to do, she smiled. You could tell she was choosing her words carefully as Andre translated.

"I understand your hearts and that you would like to bring joy to the children. If I may, I would like to tell you about a pressing need. For the last couple of years, we have only had one small refrigerator to use for the entire orphanage. As you can imagine for sixty children, it is not adequate. Would you consider purchasing a refrigerator instead?"

Andre suggested that she take us to the kitchen and show us what was currently in use.

Two cooks prepared lunch as we entered the galley. I tried to suppress my surprise when we saw the small icebox. Memories flooded my mind of when our own fridge had stopped working and the children's milk would not cool. There wasn't any doubt as to what we would do. Astonished, we found out the cost of one double sized unit was only two hundred and fifty US dollars. We ordered two, but chose to surprise Mama Luba.

With that decision made, it was time to depart.

Andre kneeled before Rachel and Luke. "We are leaving for a short time, but we will be back. Keep the pictures tucked safe under your pillow. Your mama and papa will see you in five days."

Luke hugged us both with a grunt to seal the deal. Rachel stood with her arms to her sides, allowing us to embrace her. Her birth mother had not returned. Why should she believe that we would?

The definition of trust is *confident expectation of something; hope*. Did she hope we would return?

TWENTY-FIVE

"Every good thing given and every perfect gift is from above..."

James 1:17

The ride back to Kiev on a brand-new train seemed as fast as the speed of light in comparison to the relic we journeyed on before.

As we waited for our court date, with measurements in hand, we shopped for clothing to take back with us. Mama Luba had explained that Rachel and Luke did not own anything. Therefore, we had to purchase clothes for them to depart the orphanage.

Shopping was difficult. Clothes were expensive and the quality poor. We decided to buy the bare minimum to meet their needs until we returned to the states. The Bible says to bring all things to Him in prayer. It just seemed strange to pray that these clothes would fit.

Before we knew it, five days had passed and we were back on the train. After arriving, we had a few minutes to freshen up before we went before the judge. The next time we saw Rachel and Luke they would be legally ours, even though our hearts knew it to be true already.

It was intimidating to walk into the judge's chamber, yet surprising to find a woman behind the desk whose frame signified strength. Long straight hair canvassed a stern, no-nonsense face as she nodded for us to take a seat. Andre introduced the prosecutor and transcriber who were also present in the room.

Why was a prosecutor necessary for adoption?

Troy leaned over to me and said, "I don't like this. We are not going to get the children today."

"Don't say that. Where is your faith?" I closed my eyes to pray briefly through the discussion taking place; no one took the time to translate. *What if we had come this far and we had to return without them? What would Taylor and Austin think?*

"Jesus, Sweet Jesus, please come and help us," I prayed.

We trusted Andre as he passionately spoke before the judge and prosecutor, who paced back and forth, questioning Andre with a fierce intensity.

Suddenly, Andre turned to us and said, "There will be a two-hour recess."

Troy said, "Something's wrong, isn't it?"

"Rhonda and Troy, the prosecutor is convinced that you are adopting for the sole purpose of harvesting Luke and Rachel's organs. The judge is allowing two hours to research your lives. Rhonda, the fact that you work for a pharmaceutical company has increased the concern. We need to pray."

So that's what we did.

We finally reconvened, but this time, we observed that the discussions were taking an unfriendly turn. Troy's bobbing knee indicated his yolk was heavy.

"Lord, please. I beg you to intervene," I silently prayed.

Andre turned to us and said the prosecutor had asked for a week to investigate our family. Everything within us cried no. That meant another week away from Taylor and Austin.

With a quivering chin I said, "Please, Andre, do something."

He spoke to the judge privately and she said to give her time to think. She recessed again and told Andre to be back at two o'clock, which was in one hour.

All color drained from our faces.

"Troy, we can't lose hope. God would not do this to us."

"Rhonda, we are not going to get them. You need to prepare yourself."

We sat on a bench praying until Andre motioned for us to join him. For the third time, we walked into the judge's office. Something was different. Only the judge was present. She indicated to Andre that he should translate to us as she spoke.

"I have rather enjoyed reading the documents about your lives in America. It seems you are people with good hearts. I realize the prosecutor believes it is risky to allow this adoption. However, I understand all too well that if these two children remain here, they could very well end up alcoholics, drug addicts, in prostitution, or possibly land in prison. Therefore, from this day forward, Victoria and Roman will forevermore be known as Rachel and Luke Madge."

Troy fell to his knees and wept.

The judge told Andre, "You must hurry and leave. I told the prosecutor to be back at three o'clock."

With handshakes and hastily written signatures in place, we went to get our children. We couldn't get to the orphanage fast enough. As soon as the car was parked, we jumped out and ran to the door. Jubilation awaited us.

The excitement in the air was contagious. Not only had the adoption been approved, but two brand-new, double-sided refrigerators had just arrived. The cooks were running around shouting, waving their hands in the air, while tears streamed from Mama Luba's face. Rachel and Luke, on the other hand, pulled on our hands to leave.

Andre told them, "Slow down. You have to change your clothes."

They began stripping down, exposing their thin bodies. We pulled out their new clothes and Luke asked Andre, "These are for us?"

Rachel threw her head back and laughed heartily as I placed new socks and shoes on her feet. Luke was convinced his tennis shoes made him faster and headed to the door. Rachel joined him. They ran as fast as their little legs would carry them, leaving behind the rejection and pain from the past to head toward a future of unknowns. They did not look back. Mama Luba seemed to understand as she waved and blew kisses.

Driving past old buildings, Andre said the children were discussing how beautiful everything was in the city. I couldn't imagine what they would think when they saw Tennessee. A new world was about to open up before their eyes.

We traveled to Kiev, experiencing creation through the eyes of two children who had lived in darkness since birth. Entering an old grocery store where eggs were sold in a basket and bacon was cut from a slab seemed to cause as much enchantment as if they had just entered a Disney store.

They couldn't believe we pulled their shoes and socks off in a park to play in the sand. Luke rubbed his hand over the top of the grass as though it were his first time to see such greenness. Everything we did caused delight, that is, until it came time for their first bath.

To my surprise, the word for bath in Ukrainian was *douche*, and I'm positive they would be surprised to find out we Americans douche every day. Giggles faded as I scrubbed away the dirt layered in crevices. Laughter returned when they felt the softness of new pajamas on their skin.

Our final night approached. Andre's job was done. It was time to go home.

****

We were in Ukraine for a total of thirty days. We had come with hearts open to the adventure that God had laid before us and were leaving with proof of His faithfulness.

As we stood in the airport, it seemed impossible to find adequate words to express our appreciation to Andre. He had protected us and cared for our every need. However, as we were saying our farewells, something told me this was not good-bye forever.

Andre and Troy had bonded during our time here. Troy hoped to return and bring building teams to build homes for International House of Hope, instead of just purchasing them.

Andre knelt before our children and said, "This couple adopted you because they desire to love you and give you a better life. Even though you can't understand them, just follow their direction and do what they do. When they eat, you eat, also. If they go to the toilet, you do the same. Do you understand? You can trust them."

They nodded in agreement and kissed the cheek of the last person to speak to them in their native language.

Andre turned to us. "Above all else, love, because the Bible says, 'Love never fails.'"

With that, we embraced. Waving, we walked through the gate to board our plane. Destination: Washington, D.C.

For nine hours, Rachel and Luke held the TV remote, flipping stations on the airplane TV. Benadryl had done nothing to settle them down. When our food arrived, they ate. I had brought Play-Doh and crayons, yet nothing grabbed their attention like the small TV on the back of the seat in front of them.

As we walked off the plane a lady behind us said, "You have the most well-behaved children."

"My goodness. Thank you so much. We just adopted them from Ukraine and we are on our way home."

Poor lady. I left her speechless.

"Enough talking, Rhonda. We are going to miss our connection." Troy was getting nervous so we ran ahead. Just as Andre had instructed Rachel and Luke, they ran along with us.

Customs was intense. There was a long line ahead of us and the clock ticked the minutes away. Finally, we made it to the officer who requested to see our paperwork. Each child had a folder that held documents proving we were their parents, but he didn't seem convinced. We stood motionless, awaiting the approval to reenter the United States of America.

Jesus. Please, Jesus…

Then, just as suddenly as the gavel had hit the judge's desk in Ukraine, the officer slammed his stamp on four passports. "Congratulations," he said as he moved us along.

There was no time for pleasantries. We ran to our gate, only to find our flight had already left.

Troy quickly found another flight to get us home two hours later than planned. I could barely stand to make the call home to tell Taylor and Austin.

"Mama, please hurry. We miss you so bad and we are having a party," Taylor pleaded as her voice cracked.

Those hours moved at turtle speed, but finally the attendant announced our flight to Nashville, Tennessee, was boarding. I cried.

Seated, Rachel and Luke fell asleep for the first time since we left Kiev; Troy quickly followed. Not me. I was overcome with the roller coaster of emotions that had accumulated over the last several hours. I looked out the window and relived all that God had done.

"Prepare for landing," came the announcement from the flight attendant.

My heart pounded out of my chest. Waking the children was not easy. Luke crawled into my arms and tucked his head under my neck, hiding his face. Rachel grabbed Troy's hand.

We walked around a corner at Nashville International Airport, and standing before us was the most beautiful sight my eyes had ever seen. Taylor and Austin, circled by our closest loved ones: Papa and my mother, Troy's mom, Mell and Julie (the Holy Rollers), and twenty other dear friends.

The floodgates of our hearts opened. Separation does indeed cause the heart to grow fonder. We grabbed our children and loudly wept tears of joy. The moment came for Taylor and Austin to meet their new siblings for the first time with awe and curiosity.

I couldn't imagine what Rachel and Luke must have been thinking, to be in a place where everyone cried and not understand a single spoken word. I guess it's the reason Luke continued to hide his face and Rachel stood in a constant state of wonderment.

Our family and friends were delightfully fascinated by the two little

Ukrainians. I tried to get Luke to rise up; it was killing his new brother not to see his face.

In a whirlwind of chatter, we managed to claim our bags and load into a van. I crawled in the seat on the second row and buckled Luke in the seat with me. Austin sat beside us. Everyone was talking over one other with excitement, but Luke never moved. Rachel's smile seemed permanently plastered on her face. Neither Troy nor I could keep our hands off Taylor and Austin. The tears kept coming.

Home sweet home drew nearer. We pulled into the driveway, and just as I opened the van door, Austin had the need to rip one. A loud one. Luke raised his head, smiled big, and waved his hand in front of his nose. Passing gas seemed to be a universal language.

Overjoyed, Taylor and Austin reached for the hands of their brother and sister. The little ones gladly accepted and followed them into their new home. I stayed back to watch for a second before joining the celebration. Troy took my hand in his. Our eyes met.

"We made it, Honey," I barely whispered.

Stepping into the doorway, I listened to the laughter of our four children as Taylor and Austin showed Rachel and Luke around. They squealed when they saw their rooms and beds layered with stuffed animals.

Taylor wasn't kidding when she said they had planned a party. Wonderful food was prepared with a *Welcome Home* cake. Balloons floated in the air and presents awaited.

We laughed as we listened to Rachel and Luke talk to one another. We tried to imagine what was being said as they saw things around the house with *oohs* and *ahhs*. I wondered how children so small could comprehend the transition from an orphanage to a family in such a short amount of time.

After our friends and family departed, the six of us were left to begin our new life together. To help them feel secure, Rachel and Luke began the journey sleeping together, much to the regret of big brother and sister. The four of us tucked them into bed with hugs and kisses as we dimmed the lights.

Although we were exhausted, Troy and I cherished the first alone time with Taylor and Austin in over a month as we rekindled their nighttime routines. Snuggling, we told them how much we had missed them. Their little lives were going to change, also. I felt they needed confirmation that nothing would ever change our love for them.

Bone weary, both mentally and physically, we collapsed in our own bed. I was reminded of the dream I'd had almost two years earlier of walking through our front door with a little boy and girl in our arms.

Today truly was the day the Lord hath made.

Epilogue

At this moment, I'm having coffee with my friend Jesus like I do every morning. My Bible is resting on my lap as I look out the window above the trees to the heavens. I love watching darkness fade into the morning light. Most days I rise with a joyful heart, others not so much. I just depend on His promise that when I draw near to Him, He draws near to me. It's a choice to start each day this way. I have learned that when I seek Him first, I'm prepared for the ebb and flow of what awaits.

I often reflect and wonder how my life would have been different had I not turned my back on God that terrible day Daddy died. Yet I've learned, if I linger, those thoughts only bring heartache along with a good ol' pity party. That's no fun. God slowly taught me to keep my eyes focused on Him and use all the lessons from my past to help others tread through their own muck, which is why I wrote this book.

God wooed me by helping me understand that I am His child. I couldn't fathom that He could love me as much as I love my own children. Yet the Bible says even more—a love that spans as far as the east is from the west. That's even more than to the moon and back, which I so fondly tell my children all the time.

In hindsight, I see how the product of my thinking made me believe I was someone other than who I was created to be. *I'm so stupid. The church won't accept someone like me. I'd better not tell anyone that I've been married before. God can't use me.*

"For as he thinks within himself, so he is" (Proverbs 23:7).

I now (and sometimes fail to) refuse to believe I'm inadequate, inferior, or subpar. Instead, I choose to accept that I am fearfully and wonderfully made, clothed with strength and dignity. Yes, that's right, the little girl from Bumpus Mills.

Over time I learned to turn to Scripture when thoughts of my past or stressors arose that made me feel incompetent. I'm not saying it's been easy. There are those "what if" days—you know the ones. "What if I had only listened to my mother? What if I had gone to college instead of getting married?" It's hard to take those thoughts captive as the Bible tells us to do. Yet with time, God taught me to shift my focus to His promises and away from my anxious thoughts. When I do, His peace returns.

> Be anxious for nothing, but in everything by prayer and supplication with thanksgiving let your requests be made known to God. And the peace of God, which surpasses all comprehension, will guard your hearts and your minds in Christ Jesus. Finally, brethren, whatever is true, whatever is honorable, whatever is right, whatever is pure, whatever is lovely, whatever is of good repute, if there is any excellence and if anything worthy of praise, dwell on these things.
>
> Philippians 4:6–8

****

It has now been thirteen years since we brought Rachel and Luke into our family. The time I spent in Ukraine opened my eyes to not only the Lord's faithfulness, but to the mission field, as well. An expedition with God is an adventure not to be missed. It saddens me to think back over the many times I refused to travel with my husband. I now understand it's the unknown avenues placed before us that force us to trust God enough to take the walk in the first place. These journeys bring about the most change. Can you believe the insecure woman you have read about now leads mission teams to Ukraine? Only God makes what seems impossible possible.

I was on a boat in Ukraine when God asked me to write this book. I whined and told Him that I could not write! Surely He was mistaken. I'm laughing at this moment even as I type. God does not ask us to do something unless He has equipped us to do it. I sought help and stepped onto the path of obedience, once again not understanding where it was leading me. I kept telling myself if it made a difference in the life of one, it would be worth it. Now I can even see if the Lord desires, or the creeks don't rise, as Mother would say, there will be another book.

You see, there is simply nothing that brings me greater joy than to tell others about the One who changed the course of my life. Once I removed the veil of deception from my eyes I became able to see with absolute clarity how He is continually with me, moment by moment, lovingly guiding me along life's rocky path.